DEATH BY CRYSTAL

OTHER BOOKS BY AGNES BUSHELL
Shadowdance
Local Deities

DEATH BY CRYSTAL

A JOHANNAH WILDER MYSTERY

by Agnes Bushell

Portland · Maine

Astarte Shell Press
P.O. Box 10453
Portland, Maine 04104

Although Portland, Maine and many of the places and events in Portland and in the surrounding areas are real, all of the characters and the story in DEATH BY CRYSTAL exist only in the imagination of the author. Any relation to real people is coincidental.

Bushell, Agnes.
    Death by crystal / Agnes Bushell.
        p.   cm.
    ISBN 0-9624626-5-9 (pb) : $8.95
    I. Title.
PS3552.U8244D4   1992
813' .54--dc20   92-41202
                                                        CIP

Printed in the United States by McNaughton & Gunn, Saline, Michigan
1st Printing, 1993

10 9 8 7 6 5 4 3 2 1

All illustrations including cover art by Sally L. Brophy.
Book design and typesetting by Sally L. Brophy.

ta

For Nick, who wanted a series,
and for Jessica.

ta

Chapter 1

It was my night at Pearls, in fact, my seventh night at Pearls, and I was sitting in a stupor on a cracked plastic bar stool, bored beyond belief, watching the clock and flirting with brain death. Nothing was happening in this bar—so far as I could tell nothing was happening in the entire city of Portland, period—but there I was at my post, drinking yet another glass of weak domestic beer, smoking yet another cigarette, feeling as sorry for myself as the singer who was plaintively whining her way through yet another country and western song. How much more of this could I take? Not much. When I heard myself humming "If you see her say hello, she might be in Tangiers," I really began to fear for my sanity, though it was true that I hadn't seen her in Pearls all week and for all I knew she could very well be in Tangiers and having a hell of a good time, too.

The woman in question was one Solange LaBelle. The bar was Pearls Before Swine, a waterfront dive that tried a little too hard for that bad girl image. It wasn't an easy place to find, hidden down among the last remnants of the brick warehouses, no sign on the door, no lights. You were supposed to arrive at that unmarked entrance and wonder what exciting, sexy and dangerous things were going on inside. Sadly, what you stumbled in on was only a dark, dingy, smoky hole in the wall, decorated, to use the term loosely, in phony pine paneling, neon beer signs, spurs and horseshoes and ancient Miss Reingold pin-ups. If you were from Mars you might get the idea that tackiness was a new art form. The music was so loud nobody could be heard over it, the glasses were never completely washed, the johns were always plugged up and the phone never worked. It took me a week but I finally figured it out: Pearls is where we go to be punished for our sins, and some nights we even have to pay to get in the door.

Anyway that's where I was, tired and grumpy and perched on a cracked plastic bar stool, when I heard the first report of the murder. But I was just too bored to care. All I really wanted was to get my poor old body out of Pearls before I lost my mind.

It was a Sunday night just around closing time. Linda Ronstadt was singing "At the Dark End of the Street" as she did every night around that time. The bartender announced last call and I lit my last cigarette and ordered my last beer. And then, while Linda was sobbing out how love has no pride ("And if you want me to beg, I'll get down on my knees..."), a legion of leatherettes entered the bar. Leather was LaBelle's animal skin of choice, but though I checked out each face, hers was not among them. They had brought a skittish energy in with them, like something's going down, there's a fire nearby, maybe, or a fist fight on the street. I was curious but not curious enough to ask.

The bartender did the asking for me. Picked the news up at the other end of the bar and brought it over to me. Lit a Camel and inhaled deep. That's how I got the first bulletin, sort of on the chin.

"Another murder last night. So what's going on in this town? We got some goddamn serial killer? Somebody just killing queers, is that it?"

"Is somebody just killing queers?" I sounded as dumb as I felt. Brain death is a terrible thing.

"Wilder, come on. Stop pulling my clit. What are you doing here, sitting at this damn bar night after night? Last week it was Wilson, this week it's you. I've got two good eyes myself so please do not attempt to bullshit me. You're here on a job. You're watching for someone. But why here, tell me that? This fucker's got to be a man, right? One of those weirdo closet cases, has sex with a guy and then kills him cause it felt so good. Anyway, that'd be my guess."

I was piecing it together, but the bartender was one intense human being, six feet tall and all of it muscle, built houses in her spare time, so when she lit into you like that it was so spectacular you sometimes forgot exactly what the issue was.

"Whoa," I said, sounding like Wilson. "Easy. First off, who got killed?"

"Another queer. Up on the Hill."

"Bashing?"

"They say it looks like a trick."

"Who says?"

"One of them over there works for the newspaper. Happened last night, cops just found the body this morning. Pretty messy, too, she says. So how many does this make it?"

"Since when? Charlie Howard?"

Charlie Howard was the first recorded death by bashing in the

state, the first in which anybody was arrested, prosecuted and convicted. Charlie Howard had been thrown off a bridge up in the fair city
of Bangor by a bunch of normal, healthy, all-American teenage boys.
After Charlie, we started counting.

"This year, Wilder. And in this town. I'll tell you. Three already
and it's only June. So give me something here. What's going on?"

"I don't know what's going on," I said. "But I can tell you one
thing. I'm not looking for a gay ripper. I'm just looking for a blonde. At
least I was. But I'm tired and I'm going home now. If you see her, say
hello, I might be in Tangiers but more likely not. Tell her it was a simple
twist of fate. That we missed each other, that is."

With a great effort of will I got up off my bar stool. Every muscle
in my body groaned, every bone cracked. Bedtime. But before I escaped
one of the leatherettes bummed a smoke from me. She looked too young
to be in a bar. In fact she looked too young to be up so late. On the other
hand, to her I probably looked too old to be up so late. It was a thought
that really made my night.

I walked out of Pearls feeling so ancient, so grouchy, and so bereft
of love and companionship that I even considered stopping off at
Wilson's. But Wilson's friend from New York was in town, hot from a
national conference on domestic violence, loaded down with buttons
that said "Women United in Struggle Will Transform the World."
Wilson, who is skeptical about all movements that aren't controlled by
scientific laws or celestial bodies, had been unusually animated when
I talked to her earlier in the day. Of course, she has seen more battered
women than I ever want to, many of them on slabs.

I had a few blocks to walk to my car. A misty Monday morning, 1 A.M.
The waterfront was deserted, the streets absolutely empty, the only
sounds were the foghorns calling to each other across the Bay and a can
bouncing over the cobblestones. A spooky feeling, to be the only person
on the street at night.

But it's hard to scare a transplanted New Yorker: we have our
pride. It's hard to scare a woman with a loaded pistol in her pocket,
especially when she knows how to use it. Anyway this was Maine. If
someone had already been murdered during the night, it was nearly a
statistical impossibility that anyone else would be.

I remember driving home that night and thinking about the gay
ripper and the dead man on the Hill. Dollars to donuts the story would
turn out to be more banal than it sounded at Pearls. Portland isn't a big
enough place to support a ripper, gay or straight. Not enough pond up
here for such a big fish. Dollars to donuts it would turn out to be

someone he knew.

By the time I pulled into my driveway I had convinced myself, and so, reassured that all crime was rational and that I was safe, at least for the night, I went to bed without giving the matter another thought.

Chapter 2

The first intelligible message I received the next morning came to me via a bumper sticker on a little blue Toyota parked a few yards from my front door: KEEP MAINE GREEN. SHOOT A DEVELOPER.

Some mornings it doesn't take much to cheer me up.

I walked down Danforth Street, past all its historic landmark houses, grinning to myself at that little bit of anarchism. It seemed so daring at this time when every day from every side one is blasted by warnings: don't smoke, don't drink, don't have sex, don't take drugs, don't listen to rock and roll, don't look at male nudes, don't litter, don't park on this side of the street. All those DON'T's and here a big DO: Do shoot a developer. Very nice.

I guess we'll know when to head for the hills when they start censoring bumper stickers.

Alert to the various forms of mind-control functioning around me, I walked to work, back down to that same grungy neighborhood Pearls lives in, but on the cute side of the arterial, noticing as I walked how many booted cars there were on the street, cars that were being punished for parking violations by having their back wheel locked tight in a big yellow contraption. This is progress: in the old days the boot would have been on the foot of the driver instead of the wheel of the car. I also noticed there were fewer posters on the telephone poles and not much graffiti on the brick warehouses. The city is getting so upscale! Why, there are probably more banks in town now than Saturday night bean suppers. And the railroad lines that used to criss-cross Commercial Street have all been torn up, the street's repaved, there's even a traffic light now, and the old Peaks Island ferry has been moved from its old funky wooden dock to a brand new antiseptic cement terminal. They are removing all the dark places so they can see better. They will be in our houses next, counting our dildos.

Of course, poking my nose into dark places and observing what goes on there is what I do for a living, so I have a certain stake in keeping at least a few dark places open for business. I poke around, yes, but I have no desire to change anything or control it. In fact, I'm into de-control. That's why, Wilson always tells me, I'm going to end up a real anarchist someday, the kind who blows up buildings. That's where I'm headed, Wilson says. From arabesques to anarchy, from ballet to Bakunin—it's in my genes and as logical as a straight line.

❧ ❧ ❧

It was after ten by the time I finally stumbled up the stairs and into the office of Wilson and Wilder, Private Investigators. Wilson was pacing up and down in front of the coffee maker, barking over the phone at some hapless insurance adjuster. She was resplendent in lavender linen and looked entirely too lovely to be a P.I. Considering how I looked and felt, she was entirely too lovely to be allowed on the planet.

I poured myself a cup of half-dripped coffee and sank into a chair. Wilson glanced at me and raised an eyebrow. The single raised eyebrow meant either, "It's about time you showed up," or, "God, what happened to you last night?" That is, it was either remonstrative or solicitous. I'd have to wait until she finished barking to find out for sure.

I put my head back against the chair cushion and closed my eyes. I had a complete dream—a train, a station, some lost packages—in the time it took Wilson to finish her conversation and wave a newspaper in front of my face.

"Will you look at this!" she said, jolting me back into conscious-ness. "And I remember when this used to be a quiet town. You look like you could use more coffee."

"I could use more sleep."

I was beginning to feel like one of those torture victims who is constantly being shaken awake in the middle of a REM cycle.

"Yeah? So how's your love life?"

I just smiled at her. I was too exhausted to grimace. Besides she was looking particularly awake, and exchanging wisecracks with Wilson before a good dose of coffee was more than I was up for even on the best of mornings. I should mention that Wilson has very green eyes and very red hair which gets kinky with the slightest provocation and a complex-ion often described as "peaches and cream" which always suggests dessert to me. It is because of her skin tone that Wilson never complains about the rain, which our summers are famous for, since sun turns her red as a boiled lobster and she adamantly refuses to carry a parasol.

She was still waving the damn paper in front of my nose. "Check out the front page," she said.

I yawned and obeyed. Three headlines with MURDER in them. And I could remember when the hottest story of the week was the size of the school committee budget.

"Summertime," Wilson started singing, "and the dyin' is easy. Creeps are jumpin' and the assholes are high..."

But three murders in one twenty-four hour period in Portland, Maine was a little bizarre, summertime or not. Though to be fair, only one had occurred in the city itself: the queer on the Hill. The other two—somebody shot in a robbery, somebody strangled on a beach—had happened out of town.

"Well, shit," I said, taking the paper out of Wilson's hand and turning it over for the weather report (as I suspected, rain likely) "all these homicides pushed the real crimes to the back page. Some guy from Boston arrested for stealing lilacs from a bush in the Brunswick town square. God, hangin's too good for him. Driving up here, stealing our lilacs—in a van, yet! Sells them to Boston florists as wildflowers. Wildflowers! Now our lilacs are wildflowers. Is nothing sacred anymore?"

"Wilder," Wilson said in her most soothing, therapeutic voice, "you're babbling. How's it going at Pearls?"

"Swell. I just feel like I'm stuck in some Beckett play, you know? `Let's go.' `We can't.' `Why not?' `We're waiting for Godot.' Except I don't even have anyone to banter with."

"You poor thing," Wilson said, sliding a fresh cup of coffee across the desk to me. "Drink up. You might be just sitting on your pretty little duff all night, but it's paying the bills. She'll show one of these nights. Trust me."

"She" was Solange LaBelle, the reason I'd been staking out Pearls all week. We were pretty sure, or at least Wilson was, that like a moth to flame she'd turn up there one of these nights. I would either swoop down on her, depending upon the hour and whether I was awake enough to swoop, or follow her home, inform her that her ex-lover was searching the world for her and ask her if she would be sweet enough to spare me a few minutes of her time, etc., etc.

"Frankly, I think I'm more likely to run into her in the check-out line at the Shop 'n Save. Pearls is an armpit. What this town needs is a decent women's bar."

I was about to launch into the subject of our future life's work, opening a decent bar, when Wilson answered the phone. I yawned and when I opened my eyes again there was a note dangling in front of them—"STORY #1."

I looked down at the front page of the paper. Story #1 was the queer on the Hill. MAN BRAINED ON BENNETT STREET. Not! No such tabloid head would ever appear in the Press Herald. We take our murders far too seriously.

MAN ARRESTED FOR MURDER ON MUNJOY HILL
A local man who reported finding a dead body in his Bennett Street apartment early Sunday morning has been charged with murder. Peter Lawrence, 28, an artist and gay activist, was taken into custody at the Public Safety Building after questioning by homicide detectives. Police say the victim, whose name is being withheld pending notification of next of kin, was killed in Lawrence's bedroom by a blow to the head with a rock...

I stopped reading at "rock" and turned my attention to Wilson, who was sitting on her heel, scribbling on a pad and making affirmative sounds into the receiver. "Yes," I heard her say, "my partner, Johannah Wilder, has a great deal of experience..." In trying to stay awake in bars, yes, a lot of experience indeed. But I was worth shit the next day. I just couldn't stop yawning. How did they do it, hanging out in a bar until one, taking somebody home, presumably not to sleep, getting up for work the next morning? How did they do it? Or was it just that I was too old or too bored, my hormones were out of commission, I wasn't eating enough red meat?

Wilson laid the receiver gently into the cradle, gave me a beatific smile, and said, "Well."

❧ ❧ ❧

What that "Well" translated into was that I was going to talk to a defense attorney over lunch about investigating the braining of the man on Bennett Street.

"Excuse me, Will," I said, "but the scuttlebutt at Pearls Before Swine is that the deceased was a poor gay victim of an insane straight serial killer posing as a trick."

Wilson choked and almost barfed up her coffee.

Guess not.

That was the good news. The bad news was the lawyer: Gareth

McGill, two years out of law school, never tried a murder case before. I probably knew more about criminal trials than he did. I was a practicing P.I. before he even knew there was a difference between an assault and a battery.

This was an excruciating thought. Had I really been doing this for so long? Time tends to get away from you after awhile. You start something just to see how it feels and next thing you know you're collecting Social Security. The shopping mall theory of career development: you try it on for size and—shazam!—you're hanging it up in your closet. Wilson and I had fallen into this the way you fall in love—blind and delirious. Now it seemed we were stuck with it. Some weeks, especially weeks I spend sitting up all night on a bar stool, I wonder if there isn't another way to make a living, one with regular hours, regular paychecks and regular people, if there are such beings left on the planet.

Wilson had ten thousand things to do and left me with fresh coffee and strict orders not to pass out on the couch without turning on the answering machine. I had a report to write. If I could stay awake. And after seven nights' vigil at Pearls Before Swine, I was ready to think about what the words "normal" and "regular" might mean, if anything.

Confucius, firm believer in the Sane and Normal, says that no man walking by a child drowning in a river would not stop to pull the child out. That, he claims, is regular, normal human behavior, and because it is the case it shows mankind's basic goodness and blah blah blah. By Confucius's standards most people I run into are of another species. They might pull the drowning child out of the river all right, but then they'd rape her and slit her throat.

Regular people? Normal people? An extinct species. A figment of the historical imagination. There is no normal to be and there never was. So there was no reason to change my line of work, dismal as it was.

No, Wilson was just about the only person on earth whose basic goodness I would not question. Everyone else was suspect. Sometimes I think I'm so jaded I am actually shocked by honesty. When I lost twenty dollars at the grocery store, it was Wilson who called the manager to see if anyone had turned it in. Turned in a twenty dollar bill? I said to her, jeering. You've got to be crazy... But she wasn't crazy: somebody had. How life surprises us. Of course, the honest man who turned in my twenty bucks might well have been the same man who smashed his lover's head in with a rock up on Bennett Street. One can never generalize from a particular.

Chapter 3

As arranged by Wilson, I met Gareth McGill at the picnic bench in Tommy's Park, a little postage stamp of grass on the corner of Middle and Exchange in the Old Port. Gareth had picked up two veggie sandwiches and two bottles of Poland Spring water for our lunch. I would have preferred a hot dog with sauerkraut and a cold beer, but I figured that since I was going to smoke before, during and after the vegetables, I'd wind up scandalizing him enough for one day. Maine, proud birthplace of the Women's Christian Temperance Union, is reverting to its puritanical past and outlawing cigarettes practically everywhere—soon not only will they barge into your house to count your dildos, they'll check around for ashtrays, too—so Wilson kindly sets up my lunch dates outdoors whenever possible. Since it either rains or snows here ten months of the year, picnicking is not always the most comfortable of luncheon arrangements, but today it was pretty copacetic.

I expected Gareth to be Yuppiedom personified, wholesome and well-tanned, glowing with good health, well-dressed, modestly clean-cut, wearing designer contact lenses. He was all that, but I was pleasantly surprised to find him also somewhat self-effacing and generally scared shitless. He had just come from his client's bail hearing; he'd never done one before. This had to be a court appointment. Nobody in his right mind would hire a novice like Gareth McGill to defend him for murder.

So my first question, of course, was who was picking up my tab. Because if I was going to interview three hundred friends and associates, it wasn't going to cost peanuts. I hoped he understood that.

Money, he assured me, was not a consideration.

I was too polite to ask the next obvious question: why on earth then had Peter Lawrence hired him? But Gareth read my mind, clever man. Luke Neville was Peter Lawrence's attorney of record; he, Gareth, was merely co-counseling, working on the preliminaries because Luke was out straight at the moment, there being such a rash of drug busts lately.

"So," I said, trying not to sound too relieved, "what's the story with Peter Lawrence? Tell me the man's not guilty. Amaze me."

He amazed me.

Peter Lawrence was not only not the deceased man's friend, boyfriend or trick; Peter Lawrence was in another bed in another house in another part of town all night long. Well, almost all night. He stumbled back home at about five in the morning and found a strange brain smeared all over one of his rocks.

The brain belonged to one Enrique Alzola, who wouldn't be needing it anymore. Alzola was found stark naked, but his pants were nearby. In his pants pocket was his wallet, empty except for his driver's license. He was a resident of Somerville, Mass. and had departed this life at the not so ripe age of thirty-five.

"And how is it that with that alibi the cops arrested Peter Lawrence?"

"Well, he called it in, but it took him awhile. Kind of freaked out a little. Understandably, I would think. Comes home at 5 A.M. and finds this mess in his bedroom."

"Bedroom?"

"On the bed, in fact."

"So what did he do?"

"He went back to his lover's house."

"Male or female?"

"What?"

"Lover—male or female? There's a gay angle here, right? Or is it my imagination? The paper identified Lawrence as a gay activist. It's their subtle way of..."

"Oh, right. Male lover."

"And Alzola, had he been lucky in love at least before he checked out?"

"I don't follow..."

"Sex, Gareth. Had Alzola had sex?"

"Uh, no. At least not that they've mentioned. Yet. All I've got is the preliminary report. Cause of death, estimated time. You know."

"So as far as we know, semen at least isn't going to hang Peter Lawrence. That's good. Now you were saying — Peter found the body at 5. He then went back to his lover's house. Where he'd just been?"

"Right. And called from there. Around eight."

"So he waited three hours. Long enough to take a shower and convince his lover to be his alibi."

"That's just about the police investigator's view of it, yes."

I liked the way he called the cops "police investigators." Like he was from a foreign country.

"I don't know though," I said. "It's almost too dumb to be a lie. Self-defense would be at least half-credible..."

"Actually," Gareth interrupted, "self-defense wouldn't be credible at all. Peter is a black belt. Tae Kwon Do. He could immobilize somebody with one hand. He wouldn't need a rock."

"Well then, if he was lying, it would make more sense for him to say he went home at eight and found the body then."

"That's my argument. If he'd killed the guy, he wouldn't have bothered with that story about going home at five and then waiting to call it in until eight. It's just goofy, too goofy not to be true."

"Maybe he's just stupid."

"No," Gareth said with the force of conviction, "he isn't stupid."

"He's a friend of yours, Gareth?"

"I suppose you could say that, yes."

So that explained the choice of co-counsel, anyway.

"Maybe you should tell me about him. Everything helps."

"My information's a little old. We went to high school together. But he wasn't stupid at sixteen. I don't think his IQ's gone down since then. I still run into him every so often. He's a painter, a good painter, talented, you know. Supports himself as a free lance graphic designer. Acts in summer theatre, plays the guitar, writes poetry. One of those all-'round creative people. Every time I see him he's got a show up somewhere or he's in a play or he's taking off for some bluegrass festival..."

We both spaced out for a few minutes. I don't know where Gareth went, but I was lying on my back on a carpet of blue grass with little elves and fairies dancing around me, and I was falling into a wonderful sleep. Then a horn honked practically in my ear and I snapped back.

"Well. What have we got so far? How about the neighbors? Did they hear anything?"

"No. Old people on the first floor, went to bed around nine, heard nothing. Second floor tenants were out of town all weekend. Didn't get in until late last night, according to the detective I talked to this morning."

"Next door?"

"I think the police investigators talked to everybody."

"And nobody heard anything. Figures. What about Peter's lover?"

"He's on the top of the list. Which I have right here." He opened his briefcase and handed me a file. "You can start anywhere you want, of course."

"Think I'll start at the top. Jonathan Hall. Where do I know that name from?"

"You may have seen his pictures around. He's a photographer. Anyway, listen, Luke says you know more about this stuff than I do..." (How sweet of Luke, I thought, to be so truthful.) "...so, I guess, just carry on."

"What's your theory of the case, Gareth? I mean, what are we looking for, exactly."

"O.K. My theory." He took a deep breath. He evidently wasn't too comfortable talking theory. "A lot of Peter's friends have keys to his place and he's never there, at night anyway. One of them invited Alzola up there for some reason and killed him. We just have to find out who."

"Nice friends Peter has, to use his place for discreet murders."

"Friends might be too loose a word in this context. Friends of friends. Anybody can duplicate a house key."

"So we're pursuing the gay angle, I take it. Some friend of a friend of Peter's picked Enrique up, brought him to Peter's place for sex, things got rough, the friend of the friend hit Enrique on the head, freaked and split. That sort of theory?"

"That's pretty much it, yes."

"That's the official theory, too, except without the friend of the friend. Right?"

"Right."

"So we need a picture of Enrique with his brain still in his head, and then we need to go around to the gay bars and ask questions. Next of kin show up yet?"

"Not yet, no. They're having trouble locating anybody."

"Enrique doesn't have a police record by any piece of great good fortune, does he?"

"Afraid not... Oh, yes. One neighbor did tell the police investigator that some Hispanic man had been staying at Peter's apartment. Last month. I asked Peter about that man. He told me that he was a painter from El Salvador."

"And he's where now?"

"Back in El Salvador."

"Swell. So what have they got? They've got the body in his bed. They've got him in the house. When's the time of death?"

"Between two and five."

"So, they've got him in the house by his own admission within the estimated range. They've got his admission that he waited three hours to call it in. Prints on the rock?"

"Don't know yet. Discovery's not all in."

"And what about this rock, anyway? Where did it come from? Or is Lawrence just the sort of guy who sleeps with a pile of rocks next to his bed?"

"Oh, sorry. I should have said something earlier. It's not just a rock. It's a crystal. An amethyst crystal. A big one."

"Wow," I said before I could get a grip on my mouth. "A semi-precious murder weapon. Classy."

"There's something else I probably should have mentioned earlier. Peter has a prior conviction for selling pot. Ten years old, but..."

"Please. No more." I crushed out my last cigarette and chugged the last of my bubbling water. "We've got our work cut out for us."

"Yeah, but we've got one thing going for us, Johannah. Peter is not a violent man. He didn't kill Alzola. He couldn't have killed him."

Two years out of law school and still as innocent as newly driven snow.

"Right," I said. "I'll need some enlargements of Alzola's photo." He nodded. I took that to mean he'd tell his secretary to do it, though it could just have meant that he understood English. "Meanwhile, I'll get on this and we'll check in with each other later in the week."

I shook his hand and took off for the nearest tobacco store, posthaste.

❧ ❧ ❧

In Port Tobacco, a joint that smells like heaven, my tobacco dealer, a shady type as such procurers of legal weed usually are, was studying the afternoon paper with unusual concentration.

"Amazing," he said to me, stabbing the front page with his finger. "I know this guy."

It was a photo of a man being escorted into court by two strapping city cops. He was taller than they were. His hair was long, dark and very straight. High cheekbones, that particular Asiatic cast to the eyes: funny, I thought, that Gareth McGill had neglected to mention that Peter Lawrence was an Indian.

"Customer?"

"No. He designed the logo for this place. Years ago when he was in art school. Used to live right upstairs. Worked here part time. Oh, this was nine, ten years ago. Nice guy."

"People change, George," I said, craning my neck to read the headline. Bail was set pretty high: a quarter of a million dollars. "Besides, it sounds like it might have been what they like to refer to as a crime of passion."

George made some sound that indicated he was not impressed by that particular hypothesis.

"What is he? Passamaquoddy?"

"Penobscot. With a little Irish thrown in...Too bad. Such a nice guy."

So, I thought, this is what I'll be hearing for the next few weeks about Mr. Amethyst Crystal, aka Peter Lawrence: a nice guy. Couldn't have smashed in a naked man's head. Just a real regular nice guy.

&a &a &a

Since I was right in the building anyway—The Exchange, it's called, a mini-mall—I went downstairs to The Rock Port to say hi to my friend Vicki Hammond, who worked there part-time, and to check out the crystal scene. Vicki was also a painter and so probably knew Peter Lawrence. The politically aware visual artists in town usually meet each other eventually, either on picket lines or at Lucy Lippard lectures, and Peter had been described as a gay activist, whatever that might mean. Given the context, the Press Herald, it might only mean that he was out.

The Rock Port was the size of a large closet stuffed with stones. Smooth stones, sharp stones, crystal stones, stones with unpronounceable names, stones that were billions of years old with fossils embedded in them, just sitting on the shelves or on the counter, touchable, handleable, even affordable. Kids of all ages adored this store. And the stones, many of them, were dazzlingly beautiful, strange, captivating. I could really understand stone worship when I was down underground in the Rock Port.

Vicki was off that day, but the shop's owner, Phyllis, was more than happy to guide me to the amethysts and fill me in on the lore and legends of same. Phyllis would close up shop for months at a time and go off to dig up rocks. Gone digging, the sign would say. She was a tiny woman, the better, she'd say, to climb down mine shafts, and I could see her scooting around volcanoes, traipsing through jungles, trekking across glaciers, filling her pack with nondescript pieces of rock that would burst open into rhodochrosite or citrine or celestite or Maine's own native stone, tourmaline.

Amethyst, Phyllis told me, is found primarily in Uruguay and

Brazil and Australia, though Phyllis herself had come across a vein right in Maine, on Deer Hill near Auburn, and picked up a good two hundred and fifty pounds of it. I was impressed. Especially since looking at a chunk of it in Phyllis' hand, I couldn't imagine how you could tell it was amethyst, the rock itself was so gray and ...well, boring. The world is full of secrets, Phyllis reminded me, and then continued.

Amethyst is a Greek word meaning "without intoxication." The ancients believed it protected its owner from drunkenness, so it is the crystal of sobriety. Recovering alcoholics wore amethysts. Also people who wanted to quit smoking, since its healing energy is related to the breath. Amethysts also strengthen the immune system. Gay men bought amethyst by the pound. More traditionally, amethyst is the birthstone for February.

"And, yes," Phyllis said, "I did see the evening paper."

"The Crystal Killer?"

"Yes. And I suspect that amethyst was one of mine. Peter bought one here."

"Recently?"

"No. During the winter. February, in fact, because we discussed the synchronicity of it. I was completely sold out at Christmastime and the shipment didn't come in until ...well, Valentine's Day, I think."

"You know Peter, then?"

"Oh, yes. He used to live in this building. He loved coming down here and sketching the crystals and the rocks. He must have done all his still life assignments in this shop. There's been a mistake, you know. They should never have arrested him."

"You don't think he killed that man?"

"Not for a moment. I hope you're asking me these questions in your professional capacity, Johannah."

I grinned at her. "You mean instead of just being nosey? Anybody else buy a good size amethyst crystal here lately?" Phyllis sold rocks like she was giving away kittens, only after assuring herself they were going to good homes. But I couldn't really see this crime as one in a series by an Amethyst Crystal Killer. Somehow that was just a little too L.A. or New York for us.

"So you are working for him! Oh, I'm so glad! Now, let's see. I had ten good size stones come in February. Peter took one of them, I have three left. So six."

I examined one of the amethyst crystals on the shelf. It was a dramatic stone, a good seven or eight pounds of rock, the size of half a cantaloupe. The crystals were white tinged with lilac at the bottom, dark purple at the tips. They rose like jagged needles out of a rind of plain gray rock, like dazzling stalagmites in a sorceress's cave. Beautiful and dangerous.

"You could do quite a job on someone with one of these," I said, hefting it in my hand.

"One could," Phyllis said. "But not Peter. Peter isn't swords, Johannah. Peter is wands."

Which is Tarot code for "Peter doesn't destroy; Peter creates."

I studied the crystal, amazed that color so vivid and intense could exist locked inside something so dark and dull.

"I wonder, Phyllis. Do rocks have souls?"

She smiled at the amethyst. "Well, it's made out of the same stuff we are, more or less. More silicon dioxide and iron oxide, of course, but as matter goes..." She touched one of the crystal tips with her finger. "Do we have souls?"

I smiled back at her. We are all philosophers in this town. "What is it Teilhard says? We are matter conscious of itself?"

"Indeed. Listen, Johannah, why don't you take this crystal with you. Take it home. Maybe it will inspire you." She pulled a few strips of tissue paper out and began to wrap it up for me. "After all, they believe this is also the crystal for clear thinking."

No smoking, no drinking and clear thinking too—this rock could change my life. Though I hoped not in the way one of its siblings had changed Enrique Alzola's.

Chapter 4

"So," Wilson said, emptying the bottle of Courage into my glass. "This guy hits his boyfriend over the head with a rock. The Joe Orton story without the genius."

"It wasn't his boyfriend, and young Gareth says he couldn't have done it."

"Couldn't have done it?"

"Couldn't have done it."

"Couldn't have?"

"Wilson, for Christsakes stop echoing."

"I want you to hear what you said."

"I heard what I said. Four times."

We were sitting at a small table in our regular watering hole, Shoulders, which was itself getting a little too upscale for my tastes and for my wallet. But it was within spitting distance of the office; sometimes it felt like an extension of the office, a home away from home. And here at least we could still smoke.

"O.K.," Wilson said. "He couldn't have done it. He's a double amputee, right? Look, ma, no hands!"

"He says Peter Lawrence is not a violent man."

"Not a violent man."

"Will you stop!"

"You know what, Wilder? It is a rule of life that a man will not be considered violent until he brains someone with a heavy object. The same rule holds true for a woman. Violence is more or less existential. It is a proven fact, for example, that most women who kill, kill someone they know in the kitchen with a knife. Now until they have in fact killed someone they know in the kitchen with a knife, they are not considered to be violent human beings. And may never do violence to anyone in or out of a kitchen ever again. Interesting, isn't it?"

I agreed that it was interesting. Wilson loves it when I yield so easily. She gestured for the waiter's attention and ordered another round of Courage. It is our custom to drink Courage after we leave the office for the day, Courage, the beer brewed especially for British sailors after the Navy took their daily ration of rum away. Courage, lads. We'll be in Barbados soon and you can have all the rum you can swallow. We drink it for its metaphorical significance as well as for its taste. Ecstasy, as David Byrne points out, is what we need, but courage is what we'll settle for.

We made an odd couple in the bar, Wilson and I, she in her stylish linen suit, her going-to-court clothes, all very demure and proper, except that with the humidity in the air her hair had frizzed up into a great mass of kinky red curls all around her face and down to her shoulders; and I in a black t-shirt and jeans and cowboy boots, my going-to-Pearls clothes, my hair cut short enough to spike if I so desired, which I didn't. What we do for money; it is truly appalling. Anyway we looked like a butch-femme combo if ever there was one, which only shows how appearances can be deceptive. If anyone's the heavy-weight in this couple, it ain't me.

"You've got a great profile," Wilson had said to me after I got my hair practically shaved off. "Now at least I can see it."

I used to wear my hair up. She could see my profile just fine. She used to love my lips, too, and she could always see them. And my eyes, when I could keep them open. But a job's a job. The job was to stake out Pearls and I needed a haircut to blend in. To blend in and become invisible. To trap the elusive woman who never came. LaBelle.

I got a haircut and began cultivating a tough guy voice to go with it. But I didn't really cut my hair off for the money. What money? Why did I do it then? For Wilson, of course, which is pretty much why I do everything. Finding LaBelle was important to her. The client in the case was an old friend.

So I cut off my hair. And not without reward. Not a day goes by that Wilson doesn't tell me what an incredible profile I have, classic Slav, cheekbones so intense they make you salivate, etc. Thank God my profile goes unnoticed at Pearls Before Swine.

"Which reminds me," I said out loud. "I have to meet Peter Lawrence's boyfriend tonight, so you'll have to stand in for me on the Solange watch. Or sit in for me, as the case may be."

"What reminds you?"

"Free association," I said. "I can dream now with my eyes open."

"You poor thing," she said, but this time I think she meant it.

ᴥ ᴥ ᴥ

It was clearly not a good time for me to interview Jonathan Hall, and I was no sooner inside his spacious West End apartment than I told him so and asked if he would like to change the time. Peter's bail had been set at a quarter of a million, double surety, and Jonathan had been on the phone when I arrived, sounding close to frantic. No, he explained. He had just been talking to his parents, which made him sound insane at the best of times, but, really, he was quite all right and wanted to talk to me, wanted to get going with it, wanted to get Peter out of this mess as soon as possible. His parents would be calling back in an hour. They were considering putting up their house for bail.

"Considering!" he said, like he was spitting out poison. "Can you imagine? Considering. He's only my fucking husband, for Christsakes. But, no. They have to consider... I'm sorry. Can I get you a drink? I'm working on a bottle of scotch at the moment."

I said it sounded good, and he excused himself to go into the kitchen.

I suppose there's some truth to the maxim that opposites attract across the gender spectrum, and here was an example of it. Peter Lawrence was tall and dark, and I'd even say handsome, from the photographs of him on the white walls all around me. Jonathan Hall was small and fair, cute, effusive. He was also a chain smoker by the look of the ashtrays; the rest of the room was as neat as a pin. And a scotch drinker. The amethyst crystal had evidently not worked its spell on him. But then, it wasn't in his house; it belonged to Peter.

I studied the photographs while Jonathan fiddled with his answering machine and then poured a hefty shot of Laphroaig into a glass for me. The pictures were portraits, some serious, some whimsical— Peter eye to eye with a kitten, Peter and Jonathan kissing, a triptych, their faces coming together, kissing, and separating with such a blend of self-consciousness and delight that I found myself smiling as I looked at it.

"I keep the erotic ones in the bedroom," Jonathan said, offering me the glass. "The more erotic ones, I should say. Peter's nose is erotic as far as I'm concerned...Would you like some water in that?" He had a glass pitcher in his other hand, like a gardener ready to water the plants. I nodded; Laphroaig is pretty heavy stuff, tastes like a peat fire or like fresh wool smells. A winter drink, but of course it was only June.

"I saw your show at the Brownell Gallery," I said. "It was wonderful. Those nudes were all Peter?"

"Of course," he said. "We're fiercely monogamous." He grinned at me and I liked him very much. But I wasn't necessarily supposed to like him, so I took out my tape recorder and got down to business.

His story was essentially the story Gareth McGill had told me at lunch, with detail. Peter and Jonathan had spent the day doing regular Saturday things, spent the evening together, gone to bed. At 4:30, as usual, Peter got up, went to his own place. He returned around 5:15, woke Jonathan up and told him about the body in his apartment. Then...

I stopped him there. "Is it usual for Peter to go home at 4:30 in the morning?"

"Yes. He paints in the morning and this time of year he likes to get going around 5. His studio gets incredible early light."

"You said he got up at 4:30. So what time would he get to Bennett Street?"

"It takes about fifteen minutes. He's usually out of here by quarter of 5."

"It takes fifteen minutes to drive from here to Bennett Street?" Wilson lived on the Hill too, and it only took me five to eight minutes to get from my house on the West End to hers. I know: I've timed it.

"He doesn't drive. He bikes."

"Ah. So, he gets up at 4:30, leaves at 4:45, gets to his place at 5, returns at 5:15... And you know what time he left exactly?"

"No. But I know what time he got up exactly." Jonathan was getting a touch defensive. I apologized. I told him I was on their side. I wasn't the Attorney General. But the Attorney General was going to take this story apart, cell by cell, molecule by molecule, and one of the things he'd go after was the timing. Could Jonathan swear that Peter hadn't got up at say 2 A.M. or even earlier?

"Well, it would have been hard for him to have gotten up earlier than 2, since we had guests over for dinner and they didn't leave until after 1. And the police already talked to them and so did Gareth. And I set the clock myself and I set it for 4:30."

Friends over and Jonathan set the clock. Very convenient. But I was thinking like the AG and what I thought was: what if Peter's got something going with two men. He sleeps with one of them until 4:30, then he bikes across town and sleeps with the other one until 8 or 9, being sure to get in a good eight hours between the one place and the other. Then one night he decides to brain one of them with his amethyst crystal.

I listened carefully to Jonathan's recounting of the events of Sunday morning. I tried to decide whether Peter's reactions to finding a strange man bludgeoned to death in his bedroom were the reactions of a "normal" person, in the Confucian sense. You go home at dawn, not entirely awake. You open your front door and go into your bedroom. Maybe first you put water on to boil for coffee. Then you go into your bedroom, to change your socks, say. What do you see? Blood and brains and a naked man going stiff on your bed. What do you do? Maybe somebody else would immediately dial 911, but Peter Lawrence had backed out of the room, shut the door, left the apartment, got on his bike and high-tailed it back to Jonathan's, where he proceeded to make mad love to him until the sun was really up and then told him what was all over his sheets back on Bennett Street. They drank some chamomile tea and took a shower and then, around 8, Peter called the police.

"OK, Jonathan. This is where it gets sticky. Why on earth did Peter wait three hours to call the cops?"

Jonathan sighed and looked exasperated, like if one more person asked him that question..."Peter can become taciturn at times. When he's upset about something, for example. He shuts down sometimes, and that's what happened Sunday morning. He just shut down. He called the police as soon as he could."

"Have you known him long?"

"Not very long. We've only been lovers for six years." And he gave me that smile again. I had a sudden vision of sitting down with him in three weeks with the list of the five hundred men Peter Lawrence had tricked with over the past six years. It wasn't an appealing thought.

"You know your testimony is..."

"Yes, I know. I've already talked with Gareth."

"They'll try to impeach you. They'll try everything they can: prior arrests, convictions..."

He shook his head. "I'm clean," he said.

"Reputation in the community. They'll try to find people who'll say you aren't truthful."

"They'll have to look real hard. I never even cheated on an exam...Look, he didn't kill that man. He was with me all night."

"Except from 4:45 to 5:15."

"That's right."

At that point Jonathan's father's call came in, and I thanked him for his time, wished him luck with his parents and left. If I'd talked to him for another twenty minutes, I might have wound up offering him my house as surety for Peter Lawrence's bail. I guess as a jurywoman I'm a defense attorney's dream; as a private detective I'm more poached than hard boiled. A good egg, as Wilson always tell me, but a little too soft.

❧ ❧ ❧

I thought I'd surprise Wilson by dropping in on her at Pearls Before Swine. I thought of it and immediately dismissed the thought. Sometimes you know it's time to sleep because you can't even imagine doing anything else.

I walked home through the sweet night—when Portland wants to dish out sweet June nights, they are perfect sweet June nights—and tried to figure out what was wrong with Jonathan Hall's story. Nothing. That was what was wrong: nothing. The old Sherlock Holmes case that rests on the dog that barked in the night time. But, Holmes, says Watson, the dog didn't bark in the night time. Exactly, says Holmes.

Peter Lawrence might be the strong, silent type, but Jonathan Hall was a quick, impulsive, borderline hysteric—granted, a cute and highly personable one—who would start bouncing off the walls under stress. He had smoked six cigarettes during our conversation to my two, which spoke volumes. I just couldn't see him brewing up a pot of chamomile tea while a strange body released its fluids all over Peter's bed.

So we develop another theory of the case. Peter has an outside man and Jonathan knows it. While Peter is sleeping Jonathan gets up, goes to Peter's apartment for a confrontation, brains the guy with the crystal... No. Far too heterosexist a scenario. Gay men are above that sort of possessive sexual jealousy.

Sure.

Chapter 5

Wilson was chipper as ever the next morning when she popped into my office with a cup of coffee and slid her thigh onto my desk. My very own amethyst crystal was there, shining up at her, a deadly bauble.

"Pretty," she said. She picked the crystal up with her left hand, overhand, and then set down her cup so she could lay it in her right palm. "Heavy. I mean, heavy, man."

"He must have got brained with the ugly side."

"Huh?"

"Alzola. The killer must have picked the rock up just like you did and hit him with the bottom of it."

"Terrible grip that way, though. Got all those little spikes sticking into your hand. Of course, in a fight or under stress you probably wouldn't feel a few shards sticking into your hand. You'd just pick up and—WACK!... Pearls wasn't so bad last night, by the way. I had a good time. Played the juke box. Learned the two-step. It was fun."

I shook my head; I was incredulous. "Solange show up?"

"Nah. But I met some interesting women. Don't you even talk to anybody?"

"No. I sit in the corner and read my cigarette pack. Of course I talk to people. What do you think I am, a piece of furniture?"

"Whoa," Wilson said. "Down, girl! Tell me about Jonathan Hall. And no, I have never once confused you with a bar stool. Have I told you lately what a terrific profile you have?"

I was tempted to hit her on the head with a handy hard object.

֍ ֍ ֍

"You know what I think?" Wilson said, after I'd run through my Jonathan Hall encounter.

"No, Will. What do you think?"

"I think you should concentrate on Enrique Alzola. Because I think Peter Lawrence is going up for this one unless you find out who really offed that guy. And you know why I think that?"

"No, Will. Why do you think that?"

"Because I found out something rather interesting at that hole in the wall bar last night. I am not a private dick for nothing, my dear girl."

"Let me guess. Peter Lawrence is a male nymphomaniac. A satyromaniac. Fucks anything that walks. Cannot be trusted in the same room with domestic pets..."

Wilson was shaking her head, and I found myself breathing an internal sigh of relief. "No cigar. Nice try though. No, the consensus among the lesbian community, what there was of it at Pearls last night anyway, is that Peter Lawrence is OK. But what's OK to us is not necessarily what's OK to the prosecution. Besides the obvious homophobia this whole thing is going to generate...I mean, isn't it every het's nightmare that gays want nothing more than to bash their heads in?"

"It's called projection."

"Yes. And besides that Peter is not Mr. Gandhi of the year, not by a long shot. Peter teaches Tae Kwon Do. Did you know that? Privately. To gay men and lesbians. And his approach is, use it! His rap is 'better safe than sorry.'"

"So he teaches self-defense. So what?"

"He has family up on Indian Island. There was an incident up there that was handled by the tribal court, but I bet if it's common knowledge down here, the prosecution will get wind of it eventually. I mean, sure you can argue that it was self-defense, but they get him on the stand and ask him if he ever killed anyone..."

"He killed someone?"

"Yeah. In a fight up on the reservation. Self-defense, like I say, but, shit... Also..."

"Oh, not an also, Will."

"Sorry. Yes, an also. Peter is the gay and lesbian community's pot connection. Which is what I heard the most groans about. He's a reliable source. Or was."

"So he teaches Tae Kwon Do and sells grass. And occasionally beats people to death. Great."

"Gareth can probably keep most of that stuff out. I mean, that's why they go to law school, right? But look what you've got even without it: a stiff in his house, his presence in the house at the time of death, a three hour delay in reporting it, his alibi is his male lover and he's an Indian. Now just add manslaughter and drug trafficking to that, and you can hang it up as far as a jury's concerned. And another thing. I'll bet you ten bucks that the only prints they lift off that crystal will be his. All he had to do was touch that rock once with linseed oil or ink on his hands and bingo. So what I'm saying is, if you want to save the man's ass, you'd better *cherchez la femme.*"

"What femme?"

"Just a joke. It's the only French I know. Besides the kissing kind, of course." She was staring at the crystal, and I realized I had been looking at it too. The way it caught the light, the range of colors in it, it was like a living presence in the room. I wanted to cover it up so it would stop distracting me, so I could maybe think about something else for awhile besides the fate of a man I hadn't even met.

❧ ❧ ❧

Later in the morning Gareth called to tell me that Jonathan had raised bail and Peter would be released that afternoon. Gareth also had a photo of Alzola for me, a blow-up from the driver's license. The cops had not been able to locate relatives and were going to release his name to the press in the morning. The body was still at the morgue, obviously. Did I need to see it? No, I said. I didn't need to see it, but thanks for thinking of me.

"No relatives," I said, poking my head into Wilson's office. "And how come you look so spiffy again today?"

"Don't ask," she said.

We have three rooms up here on the third floor of this cavernous and practically empty office building. The waiting room is hardly ever used for waiting customers; in the waiting room we wait for the coffee to be made and the phone to ring. Sometimes we meditate there on the pretty Ming dynasty-design rug while waiting for the coffee or the phone or each other. Off the waiting room are our two "private" offices, Wilson's green and verdant like a Rousseau print, mine completely utilitarian except for one Kandinsky poster and now an amethyst crystal. Sometimes I go into Wilson's space just to breathe in real oxygen, and sometimes she comes into mine to yell so the plants don't pick up the bad vibes.

"And as for having no relatives," she said, "you've always got me."

"Alzola, Will. No relatives. What sort of person has no relatives?"

"Orphans. Aliens. Robots."

"Illegal aliens. Peter had someone visiting him from El Salvador last month."

"So?"

"So how many people do you know who have friends in El Salvador?"

"I don't even know anybody with friends in El Paso. What are you getting at? Our social circle is too small?"

"Maybe Alzola was a refugee. Maybe... But Peter would have said something. Like, 'Oh, Enrique. Yes, he's a revolutionary and was executed by a Salvadoran death squad operating out of South Portland.'"

Wilson shrugged. Stop speculating, Wilder. That's what the shrug means. We don't even have to talk anymore; we can communicate in sign language.

❧ ❧ ❧

Early in the afternoon I went to Gareth's office to pick up the photos of Enrique Alzola. A driver's license mug shot...well, it was better than nothing, though not much better.

Gareth had also provided me with the police photos, but nobody in a bar was likely to ID the guy in that shape. Dead men don't look much like sex objects.

I called Jonathan from Gareth's office, but all I got was their tape. They were probably in bed. If I'd just spent two nights in the county jail, that's the first place I'd head. I left a message for Peter to call me and then trudged back to the office to write up some long overdue reports. Wilson was out in the field, as we glamorously refer to places like Madawaska and Fort Kent, and there wasn't much I could do with Enrique's face until evening.

I strolled back to the office along Exchange Street, glancing into shop windows at clothes I couldn't afford and shoes I wouldn't be caught dead in, picking up on some odd looks I was getting from the casually dressed tourists. In summer only casually dressed tourists and formally dressed lawyers hang out on this street. Natives avoid the Exchange Street area like a head-lice infestation.

I stopped in front of my favorite shop, Amaryllis, to lust for awhile at the dresses. The owner was a friend and she came out to chat, but I was still aware of the side-long glances, just slightly hostile. What was going on? And then my friend said, "I love what you've done with your hair. It's such a different look for you, Johannah."

Ah. Cutting your hair these days is a form of coming out. For the first time in my life I looked like a lesbian, and so for the first time in my life I was experiencing what looking like a lesbian felt like.

I sauntered down the block, past people sitting on a bench eating ice cream, past a group of teenage skin heads hanging out, past Tommy's Park and the hard hats from the construction site around the corner chomping down their lunch, and I thought about Peter Lawrence teaching dykes and faggots to kick and punch and telling them to use it, and I understood why. There was a lot of rage in the world and not a whole lot of targets for it. All of a sudden I felt like a walking dart board, and this was afternoon on a fairly civilized block.

For the first time in two days I seriously contemplated the possibility that Peter Lawrence had killed Enrique Alzola. If Alzola had been a local and had died with his clothes on, I might have put money on it.

Chapter 6

I spent that afternoon transcribing interviews I had done with two potential defense witnesses in a drug case. The defendant was an old hippie named Ray Boulanger, forty years old, decorated Vietnam vet with three kids from his first marriage, two from his current; and this second wife had a child from a previous relationship who lived with her and Ray. All told, he was supporting six children, one ex and one current wife, and doing it the old fashioned American way, through the free market system: selling pot. He had been a pretty successful marijuana smuggler for many years, the Maine coast being 3500 miles long, not as the crow flies but as the lobster boats see it, and he had brought in many tons of pot over his career. He was, by all accounts, generous with his grass, benevolent with his profits and supplied his dealers with top grade smoke at a fair price.

But two historical forces combined to destroy Ray Boulanger. One was interdiction; the other was cocaine. Pot became harder and harder to get and more dangerous to carry; cocaine was easy to transport and far more profitable. And ironically the penalty was the same. Zero Tolerance, and the draconian measures put into play to enforce it, did not make the fine distinctions between drugs that wreck your life and plants that give you the munchies and insight into the cosmos. Trafficking in crack or trafficking in pot leads to the same end: thirty years. For Ray Boulanger, thirty years meant life.

Ray had it in his head to retire, so he bowed to the times and arranged to carry one shipment of cocaine. It was going to be his pension fund. What he didn't know was that he had been set up and now what the Feds wanted from him were the names of everybody he had ever supplied in the state, which meant ratting on every friend he had. That or life.

The real irony was that you could buy cocaine and even heroin practically for a song anywhere in town. Certain streets in Portland were open air shooting galleries, but a joint was as hard to come by as a kidney transplant. They were locking people up for growing a few plants in their backyards, dismantling the entire native marijuana distribution system with one hand, patting themselves on the back with the other, while any school kid could tell you there was enough white powder in the city—and in the state—to keep us all high until the millennium.

"They" were not only the Feds. The Feds alone would have been bad enough. But we also had our own home-grown DEA, the Bureau of Intergovernmental Drug Enforcement, BIDE. This monster was the brainchild of the U.S. Attorney and the Governor; it wasn't a big surprise when the fruit of the union of their minds wasn't a civil libertarian's dream. The ostensible purpose of BIDE was to mobilize federal, state, county and local police in a battle against drugs in the state. The actual result was the creation of a powerful agency whose activities were characterized by the military overkill of a Special Forces operation and the utter disregard for citizens' rights reminiscent of the FBI during J. Edgar Hoover's glory days. BIDE's tactics included helicopter surveillance of private property, S.W.A.T. team assaults on people's homes and a "confidential unit" which collected information on citizens in whatever manner it deemed necessary. And as far as anyone could tell, nobody was watching the Watchmen.

Ray Boulanger had gotten BIDE's complete menu, the full treatment, and so what I was doing for him was nothing more than an exercise in futility. They had caught him red-handed, as well they might have since it was their own agent, one Vince Scully, planted inside Ray's household, who had set up the buy in the first place. There was no defense, only hard choices. Deals. All that was left for Ray Boulanger was a deal he could live with, and the government wasn't about to make his life easy.

One of these interviews was with another old-time smuggler, Albert Greer. He had quite a rap about the good old days, fifteen years ago, about growing fields full of pot plants up in the woods, when nobody up there even knew what a pot plant looked like, sheriff least of all. "So we'd have these two grades, right? The stuff we grew and the stuff we brought in. Now, Ray, he had dozens of ports of entry, right? He knew everybody up and down that coast. We'd just drive the truck up to the dock and unload the bales, drive it to the barn, people'd come by to pick it up, we'd all get high together, right, I mean, shit, we were all friends..."

Good oral history, but not much help for the defense.

"Ray was real lucky. There'd be sweeps every so often over the years, but they never hit us. We were operating down east, and Ray's distributors were real careful. And the heat wasn't on in those days. Different time. Course you sweat it when anybody goes down, but, you know, what were we talking back then? Two to five? People are willing to do two years..."

"About this last gig, Albert. Tell me about the coke deal."

And that's just when the cat got Albert Greer's tongue. "Gee, Johannah, now I'm gonna be just as useless to you as tits on a bull." And he was.

George Smith, Ray's partner all those years, didn't know anything about it either. Could tell me anything I wanted to know about pot, but not a syllable about cocaine. Selective attention: he didn't remember the conversation about taking the job, he didn't remember the name of the source or of the contact, where Ray had gotten the information about the shipment in the first place, how the stuff had come in. Nada.

"So this was a solo operation? He didn't have any help? Is that what you're saying?"

"Yeah, he had help. The DEA helped him all the way."

"Connolly?"

"That's right. Agent Connolly."

"And how did Connolly hook up with Ray?"

"Dayton. Dayton got busted and he knew Ray. We never dealt with Dayton direct, but, you know, Ray was pretty well known. So Dayton rolls over on Ray, but has nothing on him. So they plant a BIDE agent among us, Vince Scully, and the BIDE pig brings in Connolly to make the buy. Deal sounds real sweet and it's backed up by our fink from BIDE, see. One shipment. Connolly's got money, wants to invest. Ray's got the connection. I mean, he always had the connection. He could have brought coke into this state anytime he wanted, could have been doing it for years, but... O.K., so that's neither here nor there. One shipment. Connolly's got the bread, it's a sure thing. Scully knows the guy, and he's cool—right— so Ray takes the job and they got him. And that's all I know."

And so another dangerous drug lord is brought down by the courageous efforts of our very own Big Brother, BIDE. And how you tell these sleazebags from any other State Security outfit in any totalitarian country anywhere on earth I don't know.

The rest of the interview was about Ray's family and what was going to happen to them if he went away. *If,* not when. We were still in dreamland. Talking about the kids, how his wife would cope. How sad it was for her, three kids to bring up. The two little ones were Ray's, the oldest had a different father. Not a bad guy, though, and pretty good about child support. As good as any other pot dealer, George guessed, though it wasn't a profession with much of a future.

I shut off the tape to answer the phone.

❧ ❧ ❧

"Well, God smiles on the righteous once a century and old Ray just got smiled on," I announced to Wilson. She had just returned from a sojourn in York County; I had just gotten off the phone with Luke Neville, Ray's lawyer. Ray had cut a deal with the U.S. Attorney. Turned in his cocaine contact in exchange for a downward departure, so he was now looking at five to ten instead of thirty. Not a bad bargain under the circumstances.

"So that's all they really wanted," Wilson said, pouring us both a finger of whiskey from the bottle she kept in her desk drawer. "Cheers. And by the way, I love your profile."

I lifted my glass and grinned. "I just wish Luke had told me earlier. I hate listening to those tapes. The good old days before Zero Tolerance."

"Oh well, when it comes to getting news from lawyers, the dick's always the last to know."

"I got Enrique's mug shot from Gareth. So are you ready to bar hop with me, sweetheart?"

"Sure. Come over for dinner first. I'll make you chicken and rice in red wine with tomatoes."

"We'll never get to the bars," I said, thinking of the state of Wilson's kitchen and what would happen to the rest of the bottle of red wine. We'd wind up eating at ten and passing out at eleven.

"Fine then. We'll grab something at the hot dog stand and get on with it."

I relented. We went off to buy chicken. I checked out everybody, but despite my own predictions, Solange LaBelle wasn't in line at the Shop 'n Save.

❧ ❧ ❧

Wilson lived in a sunny, roomy apartment on the East End overlooking the Bay. I lived in a dark little house at the opposite end of the peninsula, and all I overlooked was a cemetery. We managed to live as far away from each other as we could and still stay on the same land mass. Her apartment was cluttered with stuff, including a wide array of potted plants and an aquarium; mine was practically bare. It was the difference between living somewhere and inhabiting a space. Wilson had settled in; I was still debating the merits of the case.

She opened the wine, poured us both a glass and headed for the kitchen. I headed for the stereo and put on Amalia Rodrigues. Portuguese fado music: first it breaks your heart, then it insists you cheer up and be a good sport about it. Wilson claims she listens to it once a year to remind herself that love is a lethal disease. I play it every time I come over to remind myself that passion still exists in the world, if only an ocean away on another peninsula.

I wondered what Jonathan Hall would do if Peter Lawrence went to prison for life. Listen to fado music? Drink? Find another man? Go up to Thomaston and visit every weekend? How long would he keep that up? For thirty years? And then I thought that if I were Peter Lawrence I might just split, bail or no bail. If I were facing life, there's no way I'd stick around.

Wilson came back to the living room with the wine bottle tucked under her arm and settled next to me on the couch. All we had to do now was wait for the rice. Everything was simmering away. I'd been spacing out to Amalia for twenty minutes.

"I keep thinking about Peter Lawrence."

"Don't think about him. Think about Ray and how that turned out. Think happy thoughts for one night. And let's turn off this damn music."

"No. Please. I want to hear it. I like it."

Wilson groaned and lifted her glass to me, and the phone rang. I was closer and picked it up. A woman's voice. "Is Ruth there?"

I sometimes forget Wilson has a real life in which she's known by her first name. I turned the volume down so she could hear better and strolled into the kitchen so she could talk in private. There were two champagne glasses and an empty bottle of Perrier Jouet on the counter. So.

Or as Wilson would say, I'm not a private dick for nothing.

I sniffed at the chicken simmering in the wine, tomatoes and basil and wandered back into the living room. Wilson was pacing up and down with the phone and smoking. Wilson only smoked in extremis. This call was certainly not business related. Wilson has an unlisted number and never gives it out to clients, and no lawyer ever drove her to smoke.

By the time she hung up, I was ready to cry on somebody's

shoulder. Anybody's shoulder. The combination of fado, red wine and the general tragedy of human existence, with or without true love, was taking its fatal toll. And now Wilson was going to tell me she had to attend to a domestic emergency and leave me with a pan of chicken and tomatoes and half-cooked white rice. It was all too bitter to contemplate.

"Shit," she said. "Women."

The guitar was dismembering my heart tendon by tendon. I was suffering from intense Weltschmerz, nostalgia for what I never had. I didn't even know what the lyrics to these songs meant, but I could guess. A woman sitting alone in a cafe, watching lovers at the other tables, remembering her own lost love. Third hand tragedy, but it still packed enough punch to make me want to weep.

I just hoped that Jonathan Hall had enough sense to get Peter Lawrence out of the country. Two glasses of wine and I was already plotting their escape. But true love is so rare. You don't let it go to prison for life, not if you have one shred of common sense. You flee from justice when the scales are obviously weighted against you. And I'd lived in this state long enough to know that when it came to juries, being Indian here was like being Black in Georgia. If Maine had the death penalty, it would be Indians you'd see getting fried, gassed, hanged or injected with poison on a regular basis. Peter could cross the border. He was Penobscot; the Maliseet in Canada would take him in. He could disappear...

"That was Maria," Wilson said.

"Do I know Maria?"

"Maria Santos. As in Solange..."

Ah, yes, I guess I knew Maria Santos, as in Solange. Maria Santos, for whose sake I had exposed my neck to the air for the first time in twenty years. Maria Santos, for whom I had become a walking dart board. Maria Santos, who was responsible for all those hours I spent sitting on a bar stool in Pearls Before Swine. I had never met this woman; I wasn't sure I ever wanted to.

Maria Santos was a Puerto Rican independista, arrested, charged and tried for conspiracy in conjunction with some alleged terrorist activities. Her lover at the time was our own elusive Solange LaBelle. She also had two children from a previous relationship. After she was arrested, she entrusted those children to a friend of Solange's, a woman who had the money and the desire to take care of them until Maria got out of jail. Unfortunately by the time Maria got out of jail, the trusted rich woman no longer had the desire to give the kids back. Now she was using her money to fight tooth and nail not to give them back. Solange was needed to testify, badly needed, since she knew the conditions of the agreement, having set it up, and had a lot of dirt on her friend, as friends tend to have on each other. If lesbianism, for example, was going to be an issue at the custody hearing, then Solange had a lot of dirt on her friend indeed. Solange had to be found, and fast.

When Wilson first told me this story, my reaction wasn't overwhelmingly positive. Terrorists of any political stripe are not my favorite people, though admittedly I am drawn to them. I had once been in love with a terrorist, to use the word loosely. My family had been killed by a terrorist bomb, though the terrorists in that case were state-supported. I'm not even sure what the word "terrorist" means anymore, except to describe someone who uses violence as a medium of expression. My lover, Natalia, had done that, and the men who killed my family had done that; and if Maria Santos did that, then I couldn't find it in me to be too thrilled about her case, certainly not thrilled enough about it to cut off my hair.

But Wilson had a personal stake in this thing. She had known Maria in New York when she had been with the NYPD and Maria had worked as children's advocate for some group in Spanish Harlem. Wilson had never believed that Maria was involved in the actions she had been charged with, and neither, evidently, did the jury which acquitted her. Yes, Maria had been acquitted, but not until she had already served three years in preventive detention. Found innocent after being locked up for three years in the Metropolitan Correctional Center and then losing your kids on top of it—it was too much for Wilson's sense of fair play. Wilson, as I might have mentioned, is one of the twelve absolutely just human beings left on the planet. So we took the case.

"Oh," I said. "That Maria. Not the Perrier Jouet lady."

Wilson looked blank for a minute and then laughed. "Boy, no such thing as a secret liaison when you work with a professional snoop, is there? You are wicked good, Jo. Wicked good. No, my dear, that was Maria from New York. Solange is definitely in Portland because she called Maria last night and told her so. Or rather told her machine. Left no number but said she'd call back. Maria is now glued to her phone, but she says Solange is notoriously undependable and may not call again for months. And the custody hearing is in two weeks."

"Maybe it's time to run a personal."

"Unless we luck out tonight. And, you know, I feel lucky, Wilder. I think tonight we're going to find Solange and get a good lead on

Enrique the Brainless. And then we'll come back here and drink that other bottle of champagne I have stashed in the fridge."

"Incredible extravagance."

"We're worth it."

"Well, someone was worth it."

"Never assume, Wilder. Never, never assume." And she gave me one of her nonpareil grins and led me in to dinner.

Chapter 7

Even on a weekend the bar scene in Portland, gay or straight, is dismal at best. On a Tuesday night I figured our chances of running into anyone who was likely to remember having seen, talked to or brushed against Enrique Alzola were probably about as good as winning the lottery. But as Wilson never ceases to remind me every week after she buys her ticket: if you don't play, sugar, you can't win.

I have a friend who defines craziness as going to the same place, or person, over and over looking for the same thing you've never found there any of the other times you've gone. Being an eminently sane woman, I have long since stopped going to bars looking for anything but a glass of Courage. Wilson, on the other hand, goes and finds whatever she's looking for. We're both sane, I guess, in our own ways.

And I had to admit we looked pretty good together in our going-to-the-bars clothes. Ladies in black, one with flaming red curls hanging down to the collar of her bomber jacket, the other punked out with cheekbones prominently displayed. Wilson had even spiked my hair and frozen it in place with Dep hair gel. We looked like the Untouchables. And down under at the Other Side, deep beneath the sidewalks of Portland, looking like an Untouchable was my idea of smart.

"Relax," Wilson said as we cruised through the front door and past the bouncer, who nodded us in but didn't smile. "You're so uptight I can feel it through the leather."

"I hate bars," I said, or shouted. The music was cranked up good and high to discourage talking, encourage dancing. Anyway I think that must be the idea.

"Don't think of it as a bar. Think of it as the field." And tossing that excellent bit of advice at me (like a pearl before a swine, I thought), Wilson pulled the photo of Enrique Alzola out of her pocket and strode toward the doors leading to the dance floor.

The Other Side had two bars, one in the disco area, one in the lounge. Since Wilson had staked out the disco, I went into the lounge.

They had snazzed the place up since I'd been there last, several years before. They had moved the bar to the center and put the tables and chairs on little raised platforms around the walls. The chairs and divans were comfortable and surrounded by large ferns for something like privacy. But this potentially sexy ambiance was completely shattered by black lights and overhead pipes painted fluorescent green, pink, orange and blue and far too much chrome and tinsel and reflecting surfaces. The place couldn't decide whether it was the Palm Court or Filene's. The bartender was big and scowling. I expected very little from him.

And got very little. He glanced at the photo and shook his head, which I took to mean he'd never seen Enrique Alzola before, and directed me brusquely to the bouncer at the front door.

The bouncer was a sinewy Jamaican whose real job was not only to check ID's but to dissuade obviously straight couples from coming in. The way he dissuaded them was by asking for ID's no matter how old they looked and then disbelieving that they were legit. I'd seen him do this before and it was quite a show. He could be downright ugly when he had to be, but that's what he was being paid for.

But I didn't look like an obviously straight couple, and so he was cordial. He studied the photograph for some time, but his conclusion was that he'd never seen the man's face before.

"Latinos go dancing at Blackbird's. Reggae and salsa on Wednesday nights. Only a few regulars come in here."

While he had been studying Alzola's mug, I had noticed a big donation jar on the counter next to him. PETER LAWRENCE DEFENSE FUND, the sign on the jar said. GIVE GENEROUSLY. It already had quite a number of bills in it, some five's and ten's.

"Any of your Latino regulars in here tonight?"

"Miguel. Try the pool table."

"Thanks. By the way, who's Peter Lawrence?"

"Ah, beautiful Peter. You don't know him? The Man trying to frame him for that killing up on the Hill Saturday night. Brother needs help, so give generously."

"Maybe I do know him. Teaches martial arts, doesn't he?"

"Yah. Taught me. 'Use it,' he says, so I do." He smiled at me, a bright smile, and then he laughed. "But Peter...paints. Like smokin' reefer, you get high looking, see Jah coming, God coming. Peter, man, he heals with paint. And he did all that work for the AIDS auction last April. Six thousand dollars they raised for PWA's, and he did all that himself, got everybody together in this community. Now you know.

Give generously."

There were people waiting and he had to check ID's. I took five dollars out of my pocket and stuffed it into the jar and went in search of Miguel.

The pool room hadn't changed much over the years, though it seemed to me the lights were brighter. In all the bars the lights were brighter. Dykes playing at one table. Miguel, too skinny not to be a PWA himself, was standing beside the other, waiting while a very intent young man meticulously cleared the table of all balls.

Miguel hardly glanced at the photo of Enrique Alzola, didn't want to be hassled, didn't know anything. I tried a long shot.

"You know Peter Lawrence?"

The name activated a magnetic field. The other pool players, the guys just standing around, Miguel himself, took notice.

"Yeah," Miguel said. "Sure. Why?"

I passed him my card. I have noticed that a card makes you legit, just like a photo ID. "I'm working for Peter's lawyer. We need to find this man or anybody who knows him. It's very important." It was a good thing Enrique's picture hadn't hit the papers. Asking people if they know a dead man is pretty tricky business. But this way we might get to a friend or a friend of a friend. This way we might get to the killer.

I had three extra photos with me and six eager volunteers. They'd go to places I couldn't get into; they'd ask people I'd never be able to meet. Peter was one of their own, and they were convinced he'd been set up. The whole gay community was behind him, they said. They'd get as many people to help me as I needed; they'd call in as soon as they heard anything at all. My own Baker Street Irregulars, I thought. Sherlock would be proud.

ᐧᐧ ᐧᐧ ᐧᐧ

I found Wilson at the bar sipping a beer and flirting outrageously with a beautiful young thing. So we weren't in a bar, huh? We were in the field.

"Well, how did you do?" I asked, filled with a sense of moral superiority.

"Just fine. We're barking up the wrong tree."

"What do you mean?"

"I mean he's not gay."

"You asked the cards or what?"

"I asked the bartender. Wilder, meet Russ. Russ, this is my partner,

Johannah Wilder." I shook hands with Russ, who was tall, bald, mustachioed and as intimidating as the rest of the help. What ever happened to cute bartenders? This was not somebody I myself would be likely to open my heart to on a lonely evening, that's for sure. But I'm just a girl. What do I know?

"Russ works here three nights a week and at Gabriel's the other three. Gabriel's is that really straight, really..."

"Yes, Wilson. I know Gabriel's. I live here, too, remember."

"Enrique was at Gabriel's Saturday night. Russ remembers him because he was such a damn pain in the neck."

"Sent back every drink I made him," Russ said. "After the second one, I checked him out, you know. Like, what's with this guy?"

"Was he alone?"

"No," Wilson grinned. "A woman. I told you. Cherchez la femme."

"Description?"

"Pretty, young, blonde."

"Great. That limits it to only a quarter of the population."

"No, but she had something special about her," Russ said. "I wish I could express this." I looked at Wilson to see if she was buying any of this. She was. "Like she was observing the scene but wasn't in it, you know. She was so cool. He was being such an asshole, and she was just watching him make a fool out of himself for her, like, you know, she just couldn't care less."

"They left about eleven," Wilson said.

"Eleven, eleven-thirty. He was horny as hell and wanted to take her home. She kept delaying and delaying. They were sitting at the bar, so I had front row seats." He laughed...or tried to. "I'll give him this, though. He left a good tip."

"You didn't catch the lady's name, did you?"

"Sure he did," Wilson said. Then she started singing. "Michelle, ma belle, these are words that go together well, my Michelle..."

"Enrique and Michelle. Darling."

"Except that she didn't call him Enrique. She called him José."

"José?" I asked Russ.

"José. And I'm sure it was José. Of that, I'm positive." And then he moved down the bar to get somebody a beer.

"Will, are we sure this is the same guy? I mean, that photo isn't the best..."

"Hey, listen to me. An ID is an ID. Russ says it's the same guy. We'll get an affidavit from him tomorrow before he forgets and it will help Peter, believe me."

"Did you happen to mention that you were working for Peter?"

"Sure. What was I supposed to say, Alzola's my long lost brother?"

"So you told Russ it would help Peter if..." Wilson was scowling at me. She hates to have her methods questioned. "Because, Will, I'm getting the impression that people, many people, really like Peter Lawrence, and maybe some of them might be willing to lie through their teeth to get him off."

"You think that, huh? Well, let me tell you something. Regular people are basically pretty truthful. Maybe they don't have the imagination to lie, OK? So what I say is that if you find a bunch of regular people willing and clever enough to lie through their teeth for somebody, that somebody might just be OK...Yeah, I saw the jar when we came in, too."

"Say every gay man in Portland is willing to lie through his teeth for Peter."

"Come on, Jo. Nobody's that charismatic. He'd be mayor if he was that charismatic." She smiled at me. "Would you like a drink?"

"Does this mean we have to check all the straight bars in town now too? Ugh. And go to Pearls?..."

"Nah. What we have to do next is ask Peter if he knows a blonde woman named Michelle who might have a key to his apartment. And then find her. And carry on from there. This is going to be easy after all."

I should have made her knock on wood. I didn't.

Chapter 8

I said the bar scene was dismal. Of course, it depends on your age and IQ. On summer nights the Old Port turns into a zoo which may be pleasant if you're a party animal but is so shocking to natives and other adults that we tend to abandon the area in droves at dusk. After that time the streets revert to the twentysomethings who coagulate on the corners, pack the bars, barf on the sidewalks, holler to each other from block to block like they were hog-calling, amuse themselves setting off firecrackers and are just generally obnoxious. The city tried to deal with the problem by getting the food vendors off the sidewalks, the hot dog stand and the frozen yogurt stand. THAT'S THE TICKET! we applauded from the peanut gallery. THE PROBLEM IS OVER CONSUMPTION OF HOT DOGS!

Every summer it gets worse. "And they dress so badly," I complained to Wilson. "Shorts and flip-flops and t-shirts that advertise their manufacturers, like wearing a billboard, for heaven's sakes. Like they should pay you for wearing it, you shouldn't pay them."

"This neighborhood is a summer resort. Look at it that way, and it won't annoy you so much. And this is how Americans dress when they're on vacation. Like slobs."

"This is a city, not a ..."

"Life's a beach," Wilson sighed. "Or is it a bitch and then you marry one? I've forgotten."

The foghorns were bleating and clouds were moving in low, so low some of them were in the streets with us. Off Exchange someone was vomiting in an alley next to the bar that had strip shows on weekday nights, and two men were down on the brick sidewalk, gripped together in headlocks. Along Fore Street, gangs of clean-cut college hooligans were cruising along, keeping pace with the crawling traffic, the 4x4's and the jeeps—suddenly everybody has a jeep—and the motorcycles. What made more noise, the radios or the motorcycles? Hard to say. In the one outdoor café, adults sat sipping white wine and watching this bedlam in front of them, the youth of America in all its rowdy, drunken glory.

"There are actually some interesting looking people on the street tonight," Wilson said, amazed by this fact. "See?" She pivoted me around so I was staring across Fore Street at a group of art student types in long baggy shorts and hiking boots. "The dark, sultry androgyne."

The dark, sultry androgyne was not one of the art students but was walking at top speed in the opposite direction.

"Lauren Dang," I said. "She's in marketing."

In winter I generally know every other person on the street in this town, know them or know who they are at least; in summer it's more like every hundredth. I expect to run into people I know—clients, neighbors, my state rep—and it's unnerving not to. I wind up staring at people for too long, sure that any second their faces will pop into focus and I'll recognize them. After Labor Day everybody meets up again on the streets and shares the sense of relief that *they're* gone again for another year.

I think I must have been staring after Lauren Dang because the voice I heard next took me by surprise. It was loud and too close, and I didn't see it coming. "Dyke!"

I stopped dead in my tracks and stared at him. He was one of a pack of drunken, overgrown boys, too big, too loud, taking up too much space on the narrow sidewalk. "Excuse me?" I said.

"Wilder." Wilson was pulling me by the arm. But I couldn't believe this asshole was actually accosting me. Maybe I hadn't heard him right.

"You eat cunt," he said. He said it half-laughing, half-leering, like he wasn't sure if it was a big joke or an insult to his manhood.

"Yeah?" I said, insanely since he was twice my size and had probably been funneling beers all night. "And what do you do? Suck cock?"

Wilson tugged at my arm. "Come on!"

"Yeah," he said, twenty-odd years of white male privilege oozing out of his mouth, "better get the bitch out of here before she gets hurt."

Wilson took a step forward. She was right in his face. "Back off, buddy," she snarled.

He grimaced and brought his hands up as though he was going to push her away, but he didn't finish the movement. Since I knew what was coming, I moved to the side so when he came down on the bricks I wasn't in the way. He came down hard. One of his friends made a grab for Wilson's arm, but I kicked him, with more enthusiasm than precision, I'm afraid, in the general vicinity of his groin, which diverted his attention rather nicely. By then I could hear the patrol cops running down the block, or sense them anyway, because everything broke up mighty fast, and there was a siren in the background. The Old Port is a mini-police state these days, but one can't be ungrateful, all things considered.

I collapsed onto the nearest bench and smoked a cigarette while Wilson talked to the cops. One of them, Marty Lee, came over and joined me to watch the arrests.

"Assholes," Marty sighed. "This whole part of town is turning into asshole central."

"Used to be a nice place," I said, sighing too.

"And it's only June. And it's only Tuesday. We have to triple the number of foot patrols on weekends. You know how many brawls we have to break up on a Saturday night? You know how many of these little trees get uprooted? How many windows get broken? They vomit on cars and piss on the sidewalks. Animals. You OK, Jo?"

Wilson came over and bummed a smoke. "Hey, Lee."

"Hey, Wilson."

"Make sure you report this one as a hate crime. I've already mentioned it twice, but I'll just say it again."

"What...they take you for a couple of..." He caught himself, or maybe it was the way Wilson's hair started to bristle. "Right. Message received."

The squad car pulled away with the drunken boys inside, but Wilson and I stayed put on the bench.

"This is a brutal fucking country," I said. "It isn't like this everywhere. It can't be. Do you think it's like this everywhere?"

"No," she said. "Not everywhere."

"There has to be some place on earth where men are civilized."

"Civilized," she said. "What a funny word."

"Capable of living in a city. Like domesticated: capable of living inside a house. That is, they don't piss on the floors or eat with their hands."

We sat on the bench a little while longer until I began to feel chilled to the bone. It was a damp night. And on the street no people were strolling arm in arm, certainly no men together and no women together, not as they would be in Paris or Lisbon. No cafés. No music. Noise, yes. But noise is not music. There was a strip show going on around the corner. Talk about hate crimes.

"Well, ready for Pearls?" Wilson was such a trouper.

"Will," I said, "I would like you to take me home with you tonight."

She put her squeaky fat black leather arm around my shoulders and squeezed. "Nothing," she said, "would please me more."

But, alas, it was not to be. Pleasure is slippery as a greased pig, and it slipped right by us in front of Pearls Before Swine, whose abandoned-building facade was regrettably right on our route.

"Thar she blows!" Wilson said. "What timing!"

Albino blonde and one hundred pounds in full leather, Solange LaBelle dismounted from the back of a Suzuki and helmet in hand followed her date into my least favorite dive.

"Call me Ishmael, Captain," I said, "but I just want to go home."

"Will you be all right? Just go to my place and I'll be there toot sweet."

"Toot sweet yourself, toots. I'm going home to watch Miami Vice. See ya tomorrow."

It had been a bad enough night already. I figured it was time to cut the losses.

Dream on.

Chapter 9

I didn't go home. I went up to the office, which was closer, had a bottle of whiskey in the desk drawer, a comfortable couch and the answering machine. Maybe somebody interesting had called. Peter Lawrence, for example, the saint of Bennett Street.

Peter hadn't called. Somebody named Rick had. Rick was very excited. He reminded me that I had met him earlier at the Other Side. Rick had found someone who knew the man in the photo. Remember the photo? (Yes, Rick, I remember.) They were currently at Blackbirds, in the lounge, and would stay there until closing. If I didn't get there, he'd call in the morning.(But his name, Rick. What's his name? Why don't machines have the sense to ask the right questions?)

The last thing on earth I wanted to do that night was hit another bar. I wanted to sell shoes for a living. I didn't even want to have to look at faces. Feet. I'd be happy just to look at feet.

I took the bottle from Wilson's desk to mine. The first thing I saw when I turned on my desk lamp was the amethyst crystal. Sobriety? Clear thinking? I didn't think so. It sparkled in the light, the color of rich, purple grapes, wine-dark. Passion in crystal form, that's what it was. There had to be some irony in the idea that wearing amethyst kept you sober. Beware of Greeks bearing puns.

The crystal reminded me, of course, of Peter and Jonathan, whose relationship I had elevated to the pedestal of True Love. And True Love reminded me of Wilson and the desire I had earlier to be with her. It had been real desire, too, that winsome will-o'-the-wisp, the kind that makes you intoxicated and muddle-headed. What had gotten into me? I wasn't wearing my amethyst around my neck, that was it. No. I was terminally depressed, lonely. I was sick of playing wise guy with Wilson, sick of pretending we were just good buddies, sick of buddy banter. I couldn't even remember why we had broken up. Was that because it had happened so long ago or because there was no good reason worth remembering? She had seemed willing enough to forget it, whatever it was. Sometimes I felt that Wilson was just waiting for me, just waiting, like a glass of water waiting for a marathon racer, and sometimes I felt like I was running around the track, every time around I'd see the glass of water waiting for me, but I kept on running because I knew it would be there whenever I stopped.

I was so tired. I was so ready to stop.

I passed on the whiskey after all, put my jacket on again and locked up. Goodnight, sweet couch. May flocks of sheep hover around you.

ಇಾ ಇಾ ಇಾ

If Pearls Before Swine is somebody's idea of a hole-in-the-wall dyke bar and The Other Side has delusions of being a hot disco (as well as an interior designer's nightmare), Blackbirds has greater pretensions, or better delusions. A big dance floor with tables upstairs and a downstairs lounge, it specializes in the sounds of the global village and attracts the cool crowd, the ones who can switch from slam dancing to meringue with the flip of a disk. It is also the only AC/DC club in town where anybody can dance with anybody or with nobody. I like it because it is the only public arena where I can move to music, on reggae night when the beat is slow enough for the aged and infirm and those too drugged out to slam into anybody except by accident.

Tuesday was hot tub music night for those in heavy metal recovery, so I glided easily across the nearly empty dance floor and down the stairs into the time-warp of the Lizard Lounge.

Remember day-glo posters and black lights and lava lamps? I hated them the first time around and they haven't improved with age. The armchairs and couches in the Lizard Lounge were reptilian in texture, the entire color scheme was truly disgusting, and it seemed in its totality to be a place designed to make patrons throw up. There were two couples hidden away down there, one pair close to climax on a couch, the other very spaced out and definitely female. So where was Rick?

"Johannah?" I jumped, as startled as if a shadow had spoken to me. I hadn't seen him sitting at the bar. Then I had been looking for a two-some. "Are you Johannah Wilder? I've been waiting for you."

"Yes. I'm Johannah. Where's Rick?"

"Had to go home. Wasn't feeling well. But I waited. I thought you'd show up."

"Well, thanks. I appreciate it. And your name...?"

"Charlie." I waited, but "Charlie" was all I was going to get.

"Well, Charlie, can I buy you a drink?"

"Somewhere else perhaps."

I agreed somewhere else would be better, and we went back upstairs. I hadn't gotten a good look at him in the darkness of the bar, and upstairs the strobe light was on. He followed me out the front door, and by the time I turned to look at him we were out on the street where it was also pretty dark and beginning to rain. He took my arm, which I disengaged from his grasp immediately, and said his car was right here. He guided me over to the curb where a cute little sports car was parked illegally, and "Please, get in," he said, and when I turned away from the car to say, "No, I don't think so," I felt his arm go around me and his hand move, very quickly. He pressed something soft against my nose and mouth and then the night, which was already dark, got even darker.

✒ ✒ ✒

When I woke up it was still dark. I woke up but I didn't move. I wasn't sure I could, and I wasn't sure it was a good idea to try. I was in a car, up against a door and a window. In the front seat. The car was moving. It was dark outside the window. Raining hard.

It appeared that we were way outside the city: no houses, no other cars. I tried to look at the driver without turning my head. He'd have to be concentrating on the road; no roads in Maine are straight except the turnpike and this wasn't the turnpike. I managed to shift very slightly so I could get a look at him.

Charlie was a Carlos or my name was Nieh Hua-ling. Who the fuck was he and what the fuck was he doing? Kidnapping is not a minor league crime in America. I was still woozy, and I remembered Wilson's acid comment on some cop film where the hero in a similar situation starts a fight with the driver of a car: nice way to kill yourself, bozo. O.K., Will. I'll wait 'til he stops the car. No unnecessary heroics. So where are we going for that drink, Charlie? Caribou?

The pine trees kept passing in a fuzzy, dripping blur; the windshield wipers kept moving back and forth; the defrosters were on. I was tempted to ask him to open the window or turn on the radio. People and conversations kept floating through my head. The voices were deep, male, speaking a strange language. The voices kept rushing in like waves, but stopped before they hit me. There was something underneath, soft, yielding, something I wanted to sink into. A picture of Wilson in a long white dress dancing with leather-clad Solange LaBelle.

A small blonde man whispering to me, "The best way to bash gays is with splinters of rock between your knuckles." A dark man who had to be Peter Lawrence standing still with his arm draped over a stag's back. And I myself walking through a crowd of teenagers, somebody asking me if it had occurred to me that I was going to die and my replying, "My experience with vampires is that they are always innocent. But, yes, the thought did cross my mind..."

My head bumped hard against the glass and I woke up.

We had turned off the paved road onto dirt and were going downhill. He had to drive slowly—there were puddles and potholes—and his eyes were glued to the lit space smack dab in front of him. Except for what was lit by the headlights, everything was black as pitch.

With the sort of giant effort it takes to wake up to answer the phone, I pulled myself out of the abyss of sleep, slid my right hand into my left inside pocket, withdrew my trusty little Smith and Wesson 469 and in one graceful, balletic motion stuck it in Charlie/Carlos's ear. "Stop the car," I said.

I said it clear and simple. I didn't have to say, "Or I'll blow your brains out." You don't stick a gun in a man's ear unless you're willing to pull the trigger. I'd been pushed around enough for one night and bullets are the great equalizers.

Carlos was caught off guard, which was dangerous for both of us, more for him than for me. My pistol's great advantage is its instant first shot, and an instant was about as long as I was going to wait.

He braked.

Smart man.

ЗА ЗА ЗА

I got him out of the car and into the trunk without bloodshed, threatening to shoot him in the balls if he got one inch out of line, and I would have too and he knew it. All I'd have to do would be to think of what happens to women who get kidnapped by men like this and don't have guns in their pockets, and it wouldn't have been hard at all. Retributive justice: Carlos would be a stand-in for all his brother rapists, and I would feel it was only reparations, no more, no less. So when I said to him, "You can get in whole, or you can get in bleeding"...he got in whole.

I closed the trunk on him and sat on it. I was soaking wet, and I didn't have any idea where I was. On a back road with a kidnapper in the trunk of an Alpha Romeo. I didn't even know what color the damn thing was. Red, I bet.

In the glove compartment was a flashlight and a loaded Beretta. Also the registration. The car was registered to one Enrique Alzola, Somerville, Massachusetts.

❧ ❧ ❧

I wanted to know where Charlie was taking me, but I didn't think it was a great idea to drive there. This road was a camp road; the camp might be a quarter of a mile down it or right around the next curve. A little stroll in the rain seemed to be called for.

Don't speculate, Wilson always says to me. But how could I not speculate? Charlie had run into Rick somewhere, Rick had shown him a photo of Alzola. Clearly Charlie too was looking for Enrique the Brainless and looking for him in his own car. Hence Charlie is either friend or relative. Or he bumped Enrique off himself and stole his car. Though why he'd then kidnap me...why he'd kidnap me in any event... Something didn't compute.

The road was a steep downgrade, narrow and in terrible shape, though it had been used recently. Every so often, where the road passed under a canopy of branches, I could make out fresh tire tracks in the mud.

Houses in the woods pop out at you from nowhere, so do bodies of water. A quarter of a mile along, the road crested slightly and I smelled the lake and saw the house. There were porch lights on and the friendly golden glow of lights shining through curtained windows into the darkness. A couple of cars were parked in front.

It was a rather typical Maine summer cottage, which are called camps, not to be confused with the places rich people ship their kids to in the summer. In Maine to go up to camp meant to drive deep into the woods to a log or stone or cedar-shingled cabin with maybe a wide deck overlooking a lake and a dock with your boat tied up at it and maybe a little beach, unpack your liquor cabinet and hang out with the mosquitoes. Some of these camps were incredibly chintzy; some were incredibly gorgeous. This one looked like the latter type. The spanking new Jeep and the silver Mercedes parked at the end of the road were dead give-aways.

So Charlie was taking me here. It was the end of the line. There was no other place to go but into the lake.

I wasn't feeling very brave. I was cold and wet and tired, and I was out in the middle of nowhere surrounded by trees. Another thought I had was that men who kidnap women off city streets and drive them a hundred miles into the woods are generally not nice people, and their friends are probably not very nice either. Not Confucius's model human being. No, if they caught me poking around their house, it's unlikely they would offer me dry clothes and a warm meal.

It was time to head home. But instead I headed toward the house.

❧ ❧ ❧

Maybe they were expecting Charlie, but they hadn't waited up for him. The living room was empty, what I could see of it through the window. One big room, a massive flagstone fireplace at one end, picture windows at the other, the lakefront end; contemporary urban furniture—no braided rugs or knitted afghan throws, no lobstermen lamps, no boxes of Trivial Pursuit lying about. These people were not natives of this state.

And on the table in the living room was a glassine bag filled with white powder.

I really wanted a cigarette, and I was also getting that urge to flee that Wilson assures me is the smart part of the head telling the rest of the body what's good for it. The rain had let up a little, the clouds were lifting and a wind was blowing in off the lake. The woods behind me were beginning to make scary woodsy noises, everything creaking and sighing like there were masses of night creatures massing in them. I'm a city girl and the country makes me nervous. And nervous is putting it mildly.

I walked back up the road, resisting the urge to keep looking back over my shoulder. Moonlight had broken through, but not entirely, and the world was lit by a gauzy, defused light. In another few hours it would be dawn.

And I'd be driving into Portland in an Alpha Romeo with who knows what cramping up in the trunk.

I drove until I saw a signpost. Center Lovell. The house must have been on Kezar Lake. Another few miles and I found another set of signs and a public phone and called the Portland police to inform them that I was driving in with a kidnapper in the trunk.

And then I called Wilson and asked her if she would meet me at the station and take me home.

Chapter 10

I smiled up at Wilson. She was standing next to the bed with a sunset streaked sky behind her holding a trayful of tea, eggs and Courage.

"Don't get any ideas," she said. "The beer's for me."

I stretched under the sheet, far too comfortable to sit up. The reward for a hard night's work: a long day's sleep. Now I wanted to be spoon-fed by someone who was simultaneously reading to me from Winnie-the-Pooh. I think they call this regression, but personally I think it is progression. This is what happens to us when we get to heaven.

Wilson set the tray down on the night table and started fluffing up the other pillow. "How do you feel? Did you sleep well? Are you hungry?"

It was not like Wilson to be so maternal.

"Where am I? What time is it? And you, you imposter, what have you done with the real Wilson, who wouldn't fluff up a pillow to save her life?... Or am I dying and so you're being really nice to me?"

She laughed, pulled me up by the shoulders and stuck the pillow behind my back. Then she poured me a cup of tea and sat down on the bed next to me. "You're in my bed. It's dinnertime. You have slept through a very enlightening day, and to my knowledge you are not dying though you may have come goddamn close to ending up a floater in some lake..."

"Kezar Lake," I said. "To be precise."

"And as for the real Wilson, she ran off with LaBelle, so you're stuck with me."

"How is the belle of the ball anyway?"

"I don't know. I have a date with her though. In three hours."

"A real date?"

"A business date. She was with someone who looked armed and dangerous last night, so I just slipped her a note and got her number on a matchbook cover. So adolescent. But desperate times call for desperate measures. Are you interested at all in later developments, like what you snared last night, for example?"

I made the sort of noise you make to mean "Yes, of course, I'm dying to hear all about it," when your mouth is full of eggs and toast.

"His name is Enrique Alzola."

"Jesus! You mean I was kidnapped by a zombie?"

"Right. Alternative possibility: the man with the bashed-in brain is not Enrique Alzola. How about that one?"

"So who is the man with the bashed in brain? José somebody?"

"José Ruiz."

"So Russ heard right."

"Russ did indeed. Enrique as you know has no record. Ruiz, on the other hand, has a rap sheet you could sleep on. Trafficking in cocaine is the mainstay of the man's life—or was. Now, you may ask, what is the connection between José Ruiz and Enrique Alzola, besides a driver's license? This is where it gets interesting... Mind if I steal some toast?... Does the name Ray Boulanger mean anything to you?"

"My Ray Boulanger?"

"Your Ray Boulanger. Boulanger agreed to name and testify against his cocaine source, yes? Guess who he named? José Ruiz. When the Feds went looking for Ruiz down in Massachusetts, they found nada. Naturally, because José was in a morgue up here. But since Ruiz has got a record and the DEA has been after him for some time, they know what he looks like. This morning while the cops were unpacking the real Enrique Alzola from the trunk of his Alpha Romeo, some bright young DEA agent happened to look at the front page of the morning paper, and there was a photograph of the fake Enrique Alzola whom he immediately ID'd as Ruiz the Unruly. Voila!"

"So it was José Ruiz who got brained on Bennett Street, not Enrique Alzola. Ruiz just happened to have a driver's license with his picture on it but Alzola's name."

"Right. Real photo, wrong name. These things happen, Wilder. Not everyone is as honest as you and I."

"We had the right face but the wrong name."

"Very good. You're becoming conscious."

"And what do we think the relationship is between Ruiz and Alzola?"

"We think that Alzola and Ruiz were partners in crime."

"Ah."

"Actually, we think—or DEA thinks anyway—that Ruiz was part of Alzola's organization, hit man, mule, runner, valet, general gofer...""

"Underling. Minion. Lackey."

"You got it. Not partner."

"OK. So Ray fingers José as his coke source. Next day José gets his head bashed in. Do we think these are unrelated events or not?"

"Insufficient data."

"The real Alzola shows up in town looking for Ruiz. He doesn't find Ruiz. He finds a faggot with a picture of Ruiz and then he finds the detective who gave the faggot the picture and then he grabs her off the street and drives her into the woods for a little tête-a-tête. To find out what, I wonder."

"Well, he's not saying. He's waiting for his Boston lawyer to fly in. He's going to need his Boston lawyer, too, because he is currently in deep shit. That house he took you to? That house with the cocaine lying out in plain view which you so kindly reported to the cops...That is Alzola's house, and it was filled, I mean, filled, with the stuff. Judge issued a warrant on the basis of your affidavit and they went in this afternoon."

"Well the man was nuts to bring me there. Has the criminal mind gone brain dead?"

"I don't think he was planning on showing you around and driving you home again. These are bad men, Jo. Very bad men. And nervous, too. Something spooked them."

"Boulanger. He holds out for a long time, practically until it's too late to deal, and then he rolls. He may have done that as late as Friday. Sometime between Saturday night and Sunday morning Ruiz is killed. Who killed him? It had to be Alzola. If the only contact Boulanger had was with Ruiz and Alzola eliminates Ruiz, they've protected the hierarchy, which is all that matters to them. Ruiz was dispensable. So they offed him."

"That's nice, Wilder. Just tell me then why Alzola plucked you off the street last night? All you're doing is asking the same questions the cops would be..." She stopped talking and stared at me. "Ah," she said and stuck a piece of toast in her mouth.

"Ah is right. They would be asking except they aren't asking because they already have their suspect and they're not going to be looking for another one. Why should they?"

"It isn't their habit, I admit. They're not curious. You are curious. You are therefore dangerous. You disappear..."

"And pretty fast, too. Like the word was on the street maybe two hours, max. But, shit, it's still stupid. I'm not likely to disappear without at least you or someone..."

"But Enrique doesn't know that. That you would be missed. That eventually I—or as you so sweetly put it, someone—would register an absence, a sort of, 'Well, there used to be a beautiful profile around here somewhere. Whatever did become of it?'" She smiled at me and it was, I thought, a very tender, almost rueful smile.

"So Alzola's our killer and Peter Lawrence is off the hook! Will, this is wonderful. Let's celebrate."

"Hmm," she said.

"Hmm? I don't like the sound of that."

"Well, there's the one small question of why Alzola decided to use Peter's apartment for his little murder."

"Oh, well. A small detail."

"Where God is," Wilson said. "In the details. Well, let's break out the champagne anyway on the off chance that God will reveal Herself to everyone's satisfaction, Peter's in particular. Don't move. I'll be right back."

And she was, with the bottle of Perrier Jouet, two long stemmed glasses and cigarettes. She had even turned on Amalia Rodrigues for me, to remind us that love is a lethal disease but luckily only strikes people on other continents.

I watched her move around the room, setting down the bottle and glasses, switching on the lamp. So familiar and yet still so intriguing. Sometimes I feel like I've known her all my life, and then sometimes I feel that, yes, that's true, but my life has been very short and so she is still strange and wonderful, I still love watching her, I still am amazed by her, she is still exotic to me, I haven't got her down yet at all. She was the first person I had allowed myself to trust after my parents and brother died. She was the first person I allowed myself to love. A rather unlikely choice of love object, I admit, somebody so tough, so cool, so *uniformed*. I had found one of my students, Daniel Lopez, bleeding to death on the steps of the Harlem Dance Center and Wilson was the cop who showed up first. What a love story: ballet teacher meets cop, goes ga-ga, elopes to Maine. It felt like it had all happened in another lifetime, but here we were, still together, sort of. More or less. We were still partners anyway.

And that brought me back to Jonathan Hall and Peter Lawrence, to that relationship of theirs in which one partner can say with perfect sincerity, "No, we haven't been together very long. Only six years."

And what did it mean, to be someone's partner? Yes, Wilson and I were partners; Alzola and Ruiz were not. Partners are into something together, but even steven, whatever it is, work or commerce or love.

Some part of one person's life merged with some part of another's. Or maybe in Peter and Jonathan's case, all parts. Maybe with them it was total merger.

I was getting too close to an edge and backed away. The edge was in my head. It was an idea I backed away from. Or maybe a feeling. I'd get just so close and then I'd get scared and back off.

The cork popped, the phone rang. Think of the devil. It was Jonathan Hall.

"Johannah," he said, and he sounded as frantic as he had when he had been talking to his parents. "We're so worried. Are you all right?"

I told him I was fine.

"Anything you need, we'll pay for, of course. Doctors, hospital bills..."

"Jonathan, I'm fine. Not a scratch. Really. But how did you manage to track me down?" Wilson's security had been breached and she'd want to know who to kill.

"We read about it in the evening paper and called your house right away. Then I called Gareth and persuaded him to give me your partner's number, though I had to swear to forget it immediately. Which I have. Tell her her secret is safe with me. My short term memory is a ruin."

I smiled, thinking of poor Gareth trying to withstand the on-slaught of Jonathan's charm. "Did Gareth say anything about Peter's case?"

"Yes. He's very optimistic."

"About anything in particular?"

"Or is it just his nature?" I knew Jonathan was smiling on the other end. "He says it all looks drug related now. That they might charge this other man. Though he wasn't sure about anything yet."

"And Peter doesn't know anybody named José Ruiz?"

"No. He's already been down to the station and talked to the detectives about it."

"Is Peter there now?"

"Yes. And he wants to talk to you. Hold on."

I raised my glass of champagne to Wilson and swallowed it down. "Careful. You're chugging gold," Wilson whispered in my free ear. At the same moment another voice, just as close, just as intimate, spoke into the other: "Ms. Wilder? This is Peter Lawrence."

"Please, Peter, call me Johannah. How are you?"

"Fine. More to the point, how are you? Jonathan tells me you aren't hurt?"

"No. Alzola is the one who got hurt, bouncing around in that trunk. I'm fine."

"Alzola?... Oh, right. I forget who it is now I'm supposed to have killed."

Smooth. Very intense, and very smooth. A phone-sex voice if ever there was one. I told him it might be a good idea for us to meet and he agreed and we made a date to get together at the civilized hour of ten-thirty. At his studio perhaps? There was a pause and then he said, "I haven't been back there yet," and he sounded like I had touched a wound. So we'd meet at Jonathan's. That was fine. I thanked him for calling, and he thanked me for everything I had done for them. He resisted the use of the singular, or he just didn't think in the singular. I wished them both a goodnight.

"Maybe marriages *are* made in heaven," I said to Wilson, this time sipping the champagne she poured into my glass.

"Hmm."

"Some people find their other half and some people don't."

"Yeah. Or some people find their other half and decide they don't like it. Wrong sex, wrong color, too skinny, too fat, terrible taste in..."

"Will..." I was about to enter dangerous territory, the zone of the unspeakable, "...remember when we first met? I was just thinking about that."

"The hottest summer in New York City history I believe it was."

"And then we came up here?"

"To cool off."

"We lived together."

"I seem to remember."

"Then I got scared. That's what happened, isn't it?"

"Yes."

"What was I scared of?"

"Tragedy," she said.

"You knew that?"

"Yes."

"Why didn't you tell me?"

"That you were scared? What good would it have done? You can't talk somebody out of being scared."

"What do you do then?"

"You leave," she said, refilling our glasses with bubbles and smiling more to herself, I thought, than at me. "Or you wait."

A little while later Wilson had to go out to meet LaBelle. I wasn't up for any more adventures. I went home and went back to sleep.

Chapter 11

First thing in the morning I called Dave St. John, the detective in charge of the Ruiz murder, and asked him if I could get a look at Peter Lawrence's apartment. We made an appointment for one o'clock. Then I called Luke Neville, Ray Boulanger's attorney, and sweet-talked his secretary into squeezing me in to see him before the end of the decade. And what, I asked her, did Luke think would happen to Ray's deal with the government now that Ruiz was dead? No good testifying against a dead man. No, she said, but Luke was confident that the deal would hold.

"They made a bargain, and the U.S. Attorney already approved their motion for a departure."

"And when did that happen?"

"Monday morning."

"Hmm," I said.

"Lucky man," she said brightly.

Lucky indeed. Not only does Ruiz turn up dead, but he turns up dead with somebody else's name. Ray Boulanger was born under a lucky star for sure.

&a &a &a

After seeing him in black and white and in various stages of undress and hearing him described as everything from healer to reservation tough, I was eager indeed to meet Peter Lawrence in the flesh. I wasn't disappointed. Yes, as in Jonathan's photographs, he looked one hundred percent Penobscot, but the Celt genes were in there too, manifesting themselves in charm and probably in blarney, if I were sharp enough to detect it. He was certainly as handsome in person as in those photographs, a long-haired, long-nosed, high cheekboned, brown skinned, barefoot Native American in blue jeans and a workshirt. No wonder no one in his or her right mind could imagine him bashing someone to death with a rock.

But I had spent my formative years around handsome ballet dancers, most of whom were utterly charming and just as many of whom I could easily imagine bashing someone to death with a rock. In fact, I had witnessed bashings of all kinds, in and out of dressing rooms, on railway platforms, backstage, even in the wings just before the curtain went up. I've seen dancers go after each other with sharp instruments, slap each other's faces, throw temper tantrums that would put a two year old to shame. But this train of thought was sheer defensiveness. Peter Lawrence was the sort of man I was born to like, and I hate knowing I'm going to like someone in advance. I like to be amazed.

His story followed Jonathan's chapter and verse. Except he could tell me how it felt to walk into his bedroom and find a dead man on his bed. Not surprisingly it didn't feel too good.

"Did you go into the room?"

"No. I opened the door, saw the body and left." He spoke haltingly as though he remembered everything too vividly and needed to take long breaths between images.

"You didn't check to see if he was alive or dead?"

His look managed to combine both horror and pity. "I could see enough from where I stood to know he was dead."

"You do have a phone in the apartment?"

"Yes."

"What room is it in?"

"The studio. So I can reach it."

"And it didn't cross your mind to call the cops from there?"

He paused a moment, thinking. "No, to tell you the truth, it didn't. All I could think of was leaving that place and getting back to Jonathan."

I offered him a cigarette. He said he didn't smoke. I am well trained and asked him if he minded if I did. He laughed.

"But you've met Jonathan," he said. "How could I mind?"

"He smokes more than I do," I said, glad for a small reprieve from the interrogation.

"Yes. I keep telling him it's not a good time to be either a smoker or a pedophile. He tells me I should just be thankful he's not both."

"I understand you've been working quite a lot with the AIDS Center. That you organized the auction last spring."

"Well, I did some hustling for the auction, yes. Donated some pieces. It's the least I could do. I mean that, seriously. I'm very selfish about my time. The person who really gives himself to the PWA Project is Jonathan. He's been making photographs of people, before they get sick. For their lovers or parents or kids. He puts so much into those photographs—it stuns me to watch him at it. It's because he's so aware that he is making the last image of that particular man, it becomes so important to him, to convey the spirit behind the appearance, to capture the essence of that person. And it's so difficult, it takes such empathy, such surrender. It exhausts him. But, you know, there's something..." He was searching for the word, and I realized that he was one of those rare people who actually chose his words rather than letting them fall willy-nilly out of his mouth, "...heroic, fearless, about those portraits. And there are other artists, too, working with PWA's, helping them create their own last work... God, it must be so terrifying making something and knowing it will be the last thing you make in this world. The last gift you give... So, comparatively speaking, hustling some work and making some phone calls...it's no big deal, you know."

Cigarette break was over. I got us back on track. Had he touched anything in the apartment before he left? No.

"The amethyst crystal, Peter...was it yours?"

"Yes."

"Where was it kept?"

"Actually," he said a bit sheepishly, "I used it for a doorstop."

"In the bedroom?"

"Yes."

"So it would have been on the floor by the door?"

"That's right."

"How big is it exactly?"

"Weighed about five pounds. Fit pretty snugly in the palm of my hand." He opened his hand for me, palm up. It was a big hand. "Amethyst strengthens the immune system, among other things. It's the gay crystal. And purple, too. Of course." There was irony in his voice or maybe a bit of self-mockery. His voice was telling me one thing, but his eyes were saying something else. They were black, slanted at the corners, and they were not ironic, not mocking. There was a wariness in his look, as though he were observing me much more carefully than I was observing him. He was like an amiable host who is half-convinced his guest is planning to walk off with the silverware.

"Let's just go over the entrances and exits," I said. To my surprise he started to smile, he did smile, he might even have laughed except that he caught himself. I didn't get what was so amusing but I carried on. "You have a downstairs front door and the door to your apartment. Do you have back doors, too?"

"Yes."

"Which door did you come in that morning?"

"The back. I usually come in the back. I leave my bike on the back porch. It's safer there."

"Are the downstairs doors kept locked?"

"The front is generally. The back is always left open. I don't think I even have a key to the downstairs back door."

"What about your apartment doors?"

"Same thing. The front door is usually locked and the back isn't. Well, we learned that lesson. Jonathan has been putting new locks on everything for the past few days."

"How is your family dealing with all this?"

"Well, Jonathan's been wonderful, of course. His parents put their house up for the surety bond. They're very supportive."

"And your parents?"

"My parents are both dead," he said. It's the sentence that, if nothing else, is guaranteed to win me over heart and soul. And I almost thought that he was reading it on my face and that he was going to say he was so sorry, so very sorry, and how had it happened, but he didn't. (They were killed by a car bomb. And yours?) Instead he asked me if I'd like another cup of tea.

"I don't see the rest of my family much," he said, re-filling my cup. It was Irish Breakfast tea; one took it, naturally, with milk. "Jonathan's my only real link to that world."

"What world?" Jonathan didn't look Penobscot to me.

"Oh, you know," he said, smiling at me. "Family. Home. Regular meals."

He stretched his legs, and I was reminded of how tall he was. Muscular, too. Strong. I hadn't read the coroner's report, but I had gathered that Ruiz's skull had been pretty pulverized by that rock. It would take some strength to damage a man's head like that.

"Ruiz was a cocaine dealer. I suppose they told you that."

"Yes. We went through the cocaine question at length down at the Bastille. Oh, excuse me, the Public Safety Building."

"You don't know any cocaine dealers? Remember, I'm your friendly private detective, Peter. Not the Inquisition."

"I'll tell you. I know a lot of people and some of them are users. Now some of them may also be dealers...but not so far as I know."

"Do you know a woman named Michelle? Pretty, blonde?"

He furrowed his brow for a few seconds. "I know someone named Michelle, but she isn't blonde."

"Might she have a key to your apartment?"

"I thought we just realized a key wasn't necessary. But she might have a key. She's a photographer. Lives on Peaks Island. Michelle Garner."

"Peter, this is important. I want you to think about this. Is there anyone who might have it in for you in a serious way? Anybody? Maybe a small time dealer with ties to bigger fish, somebody who might want to set you up? You've sold a little pot in this town. So maybe you walked on somebody's toes and they want you out of the picture... Because our problem right now is this. Say Alzola killed Ruiz, OK? Why did he kill him in your apartment?"

He said he'd think about it, but that off-hand nobody came to mind. He said he didn't think he had any enemies, not personal enemies. He said he did speak up for things some people found offensive, but that he really didn't think that the Christian right in this state would shack up with the likes of Enrique Alzola, old saws about politics making strange bedfellows notwithstanding.

He was by far the calmest, most relaxed murder suspect I had ever interviewed.

I asked him if he knew the bars were collecting money for his defense fund. He hadn't heard, and he looked half-embarrassed and half-pleased. "Maybe we'll be lucky and I won't need a defense fund," he said.

"How lucky are you, generally?" I asked, gathering my things together, getting ready to leave. What I was really thinking was, I have one lucky client. I'm not sure I'm eligible for two.

"Well, I've tested negative and Jonathan's tested negative so I guess I'm pretty goddamn lucky. And you, Johannah, how lucky are you?"

He was smiling, but there was a challenge there somewhere, like an invisible gauntlet had just been thrown at my feet. Luck, Wilson says, is just another kind of smart. So how smart were we? That was the question.

❧ ❧ ❧

Bennett Street ran north-south along the crest of Munjoy Hill. It was a working class neighborhood of wooden three-flats, some with sideyards, most without. The Hill wasn't lacking in trees and gardens, but the trees were mostly along the perimeter, in the park called the Eastern Promenade, and the gardens were mostly small and adorned with statues of St. Anthony or what Wilson called Bathtub Madonnas, an old tub, set upright, serving as the shrine. The streets weren't clean, but they weren't filthy. On Bennett Street itself little kids were playing in the dirt, having a ball at it, like sparrows taking dirt baths, and older kids were riding bikes up and down the sidewalks. It was a hot day for June and the sparkling blue water of Casco Bay looked particularly inviting, though I knew, like these kids did, that it would be cold as ice.

Detective St. John gave me the key and a wave up. He was just as happy to wait for me outside and read the paper, had no desire to watch me poke around. And I didn't even know what I was poking around for. "Fifteen minutes," I said. "Hey," he answered, "take twenty. Hell, you got Lawrence's permission. I don't even need to be here. We're done with this place." But he waited anyway, because, in fact, they weren't really sure they were done with the place, and he was the obliging sort and was dying to read the sports section.

It was as though no one really lived in this apartment at all. It was Peter's studio space and he could make coffee there. And besides paint and drink coffee it didn't seem that he did much else.

The front door opened onto a living room. There was a battered old couch, a good stereo system. Nothing else.

The former dining room was his studio. A wall of windows faced south, and since he was on the third floor and his building had a side yard separating it from its neighbors he had an unblocked view of the bay. Unblocked light.

The floor was covered with newspapers and the tools of his trade: tubes of oils, cans of turpentine and linseed oil, palette knives and brushes, some soaking in old coffee cans. Canvasses were stacked along one wall; several were hanging. But the strangest thing to my eye was that the one he must have been most recently working on, the one on the easel in the middle of the room, was draped with a white sheet.

I left it alone and looked at the others, the ones hanging on the walls and the ones stacked on the side of the room. They were big canvasses, long rather than wide, long and lean, 72x36, 84x48, all variations on the same theme: long lines forming almost sculptural shapes like elongated mythical animals, but Watusi size. Then that linear element combined with a geometric, so the lines grew into triangles. Finally the geometric evolved further, into form; the lines became erotic bodies enfolding each other, supporting each other, laughing with each other. The humor was there, the wit, but it was a part of a larger energy in the work, and that energy was a combination of movement and color and light. Color was chosen with the same concentration as he chose words: it was used sparingly but when it was, it was either muted or intense. The paintings were like other presences in the room.

Like seeing Jah, the bouncer had said.

The one he had been working on, the one that was draped, that one in particular had such inner light. But it had been covered wet, and the sheet had caused the paint to smear.

I went back to the living room and sat down on the couch. Two room lengths away, fifteen, twenty feet, that's how far you had to be to see the paintings properly. This is where Peter would sit. He would paint and then he would sit here. He would smoke a joint and look at what he had done. And, yes, as I expected, there was an ashtray on the floor, just slightly under the couch, right within arm's reach of where I was sitting.

On the other side of the dining room was the kitchen. It wasn't a working kitchen. All Peter cooked here was coffee. There were a few Pepsis in the refrigerator, orange juice, water.

Then off the kitchen, the bedroom.

A double mattress on the floor, stripped. They must have removed the bedclothes for evidence. A guitar standing in the corner. A closet, door ajar: jackets, a few shirts. A desk with pens, drawing paper. Over the desk, hanging on the wall, a drawing. Made with crayons. Flowers, trees, animals, a big yellow sun, a rainbow, and a small figure up front holding a bouquet. A child's drawing.

Printed in big black letters on the top were the words: HAPPY DAY PAPA I LOVE YOU. On the bottom: FROM ME Beneath those words were a few very well drawn fish and following in the fish's wake and in emerald green crayon the name ZOE NEPTUNE.

No one had mentioned to me that Peter Lawrence had a child.

I walked back through the kitchen and the studio toward the front door. There was a poster tacked up to it, announcing a local theatre company's production of *Rosencranz and Gildenstern Are Dead*. I wondered what it was doing on Peter's door. Maybe he had designed it. Then I looked at it more carefully. It wasn't because of the design that it was hanging up. I had completely forgotten that among all the other things Peter Lawrence was, he was also an actor.

❧ ❧ ❧

St. John was still immersed in the sports section. I returned the house keys and thanked him.

"Can I ask you a couple of questions?

"Ask away."

"Did you find any drugs up there?"

"Place was clean as a whistle."

"Not even a roach in an ashtray?"

"Not even a seed."

"How come you covered the painting?"

"Didn't. Came that way."

"And the mattress...there's no blood on the mattress."

"No. Talk to forensic. They got everything out of there they needed."

"So that's all you took? Sheets, pillows?"

"Victim's clothes. Shoes... You want to see the evidentiary list, McGill's got it."

"And you're sure nobody covered that painting?"

He shook his head and started the car. Now that he'd caught up on the baseball scores, he was too busy to waste his time on dumb questions about draped canvasses and empty ashtrays.

Chapter 12

Wilson was on the phone again and pacing. I sat on her desk and watched. It was the Maria Santos pace. She gestured for a cigarette. Ah, yes. Must be Maria Santos.

I had discovered some intriguing things about Peter Lawrence: that he owned an ashtray but didn't smoke; dealt grass but kept a drug-free house; was gay but had a child; and draped wet canvasses with sheets before he left them for the night. All this struck me as uncommonly odd, but I was sure that Wilson would make sense of it. Peter doesn't smoke but Jonathan does; he doesn't keep his stash in the studio, he's got a stash house like any smart dealer; many gay men have been known to father children, though they called themselves bisexual at the time (and, Wilder, as you well know, we're all bisexual until we shack up with somebody), and many artists probably drape their paintings the way canary owners drape their cages.

Sure, Wilson, I'd answer her, but unfinished paintings? Oil paintings? There was paint on that sheet from the painting; the work had been damaged. Why would he do that? Why would a painter cover a wet painting with a sheet?

"Ugh," Wilson said, hanging up the phone. "She deeked me."

"What?"

"LaBelle. She deeked me last night."

"Deeked you? Is that some kind of weird sexual act?"

"Stood me up. Didn't show. Wasn't there. I went to her house this morning, and her roommate says she's out of town for the weekend. Like I almost believe it. Went to P'town, says the roommate."

"And you don't believe it? Provincetown is lovely this time of year. Anyway, she'll be back."

"Meanwhile Maria's going nuts. We're running out of time on this one."

"Why doesn't Maria just subpoena her?"

"Oh, right. All she needs is a hostile witness."

"Well, we'll talk her into it. Don't worry."

"We'll never talk her into anything if we can't fucking find her. It's so frustrating..."

"Come on, honey," I said in what I hoped was a soothing voice. "Let me buy you some Courage."

❧ ❧ ❧

We strolled into Shoulders at just half past four, and there standing at the bar were none other than old Luke and young Gareth. "My, my," Wilson said. "Lawyers in love. Let's buy them a beer and pick their brains."

I wasn't sure I could handle two lawyers at once, but luckily young Gareth couldn't stay, had to go home, probably to shine up his BMW. But Luke joined us. Luke is constitutionally unable to turn down a free beer.

Luke Neville was one of the few lawyers in town I actually enjoyed working for. He had two legendary claims to fame. He had been the first lawyer in Portland to wear Bean boots into court and get away with it, thus starting a trend twenty years in advance of its time for eccentricity among the Maine bar; one of the DA's now wears red sneakers to court and owes it all to Luke's path finding efforts back in the early pioneer days. And he had once brought his eldest son to court with him to watch a trial and introduced him afterwards to the DA and even the judge, which would have been no big deal except that at the time his son sported a bright orange Mohawk.

"Old flower children never die," he said to me once. "We just go to seed."

"How's Ray these days?" I asked him after he had taken a few sips of his Bass and swapped a few court jokes with Wilson.

"Relieved," he said. "We're all relieved."

"I suppose eight to ten's no picnic. But it beats thirty by half a lifetime."

"Well, it's even more dramatic than that. Ray was scared, but not of thirty years. He's been under an incredible amount of pressure. The Mafia had threatened him. Heavy shit. Very heavy shit."

"I didn't know anything about that...What mafia?"

"The drug Mafia. The Medellin Mafia. Whoever they are, wherever they come from. They called Ray's wife after the bust, told her if Ray rolled on them, they'd come after her and the kids. And they were not kidding. These people do not kid around. They knew the children's names, ages, where they went to school, who babysat for them and when. Scared the shit out of her. But do you think the DEA *believed* her? Do you think they *cared*? A bunch of vindictive, mean spirited bastards. They will weigh the *paper* that blotter acid comes on so they can up the aggregate weight for sentencing. They will weigh the entire marijuana plant, roots and all, to up the aggregate weight. So what would be an ounce of usually very poor home grown turns into pounds. How to turn a civil offense into a felony. Our law enforcement officers are very often deceptive. Not only that, they are without honor. And absolutely merciless. See what they did to the Dogman? Busted him, took his dogs away...what harm's he doing anyone? What's the harm of walking around with ten dogs around you? So he was a little loud... Now you think BIDE or the DEA gives a flying fuck if José Ruiz and his ilk threaten citizens of this state? Hell, no. Ray should have thought of that before he got mixed up with them. Lie down with dogs—to maintain the metaphor (I know you appreciate these touches, Jo)—get up with fleas. Yes, indeed. And it will deter others! One of those bastards actually said that to me. Vince Scully, in fact, the BIDE agent that set Ray up, and he knows those people, he practically lived with those people, those children, and he says that to me. It will deter others, a dead woman and a few dead kids up there in Washington County...it will deter others!

"So, this is why I practice law, ladies. To keep those motherfuckers honest. To watch them like Jehovah himself. They get one little comma out of place on a warrant, man, I'm on their case. Because they are little fascists, most of them—not all, but most—and they must be controlled... Any other questions?"

"Another Bass, Luke?"

"How about a cigarette, Luke?"

"Yup to the first. Yup to the second. And what do you want to know?"

"Our current working hypothesis is that Alzola killed Ruiz," Wilson said. "The only snag we haven't quite worked out is why he did it in Peter Lawrence's apartment."

"Interesting. It's not a typical Mafia killing, I'll tell you that much. But you never know. Maybe they're getting a little more sophisticated. If Alzola wanted to terminate Ruiz but knew Ruiz had friends who might not take it well, he might want to disguise it, make it look like a gay thing. Could be a clever move. But are they that clever? That's the question."

"Are you still co-counseling with Gareth on that case?"

"We were just discussing that. I think it has the semblance of impropriety, representing one client accused of killing another client's cocaine source. And it might turn into an outright conflict if Boulanger should come into it in any way. Though since he was in the custody of the Department of Corrections at the time, it seems highly unlikely. So, no, I'm not co-counseling. But I agree with Gareth that he's got a good shot at acquittal now. Lawrence may not even get indicted. He's got a tight alibi, no motive, no priors. But you never know about grand juries. The gay angle has its appeal."

"They have to prosecute somebody," Wilson said. "And they have a somebody, gay and Indian, no less. Oh, it has its appeal all right."

"The grand jury still needs evidence," I said.

"Grand juries, in my experience, usually do what they're told," Luke said. "Luckily from what I understand, forensics did not find any traces of semen on, in or near José Ruiz's body. Not even on the sheets. Because with DNA tracing... Well, it's not an issue so why worry about it. Now let me ask you, are you two out straight at the moment or could I get you to do a little work for me on this Bridgton murder? Hear about it? Guy shot in the woods last weekend?"

"Robbery, wasn't it?" Wilson said.

"At half glance, maybe. OK. This dumb kid tells his girlfriend he's going to waste some guy for ripping him off in a drug deal. Even shows her the gun he's going to use. Two days later the guy's dead. Robbed in the woods. Like somebody's gonna believe that. Only problem the state police have is that the guy was shot with a nine millimeter and the gun my client showed his girlfriend was a shotgun. The nine millimeter hasn't shown up yet. Also the victim was...well, mutilated is the word that's used. Butchered is more like it... Not a pretty sight. And the coroner seems to think that the bullets finished him off, if you get my drift." He took a long swallow of his ale. "I have a pretty strong stomach, but I couldn't finish reading the coroner's report."

"What do you need us for?"

"Checking alibis. Talking to girlfriends. I've represented this kid before. He's pretty much an asshole, but he's a normal asshole, know what I mean? Torture slayings are not in his repertory."

"Well, we have time, don't we, Wilder?" Wilson said brightly. "Another drug-related killing in Maine. This just may stem the on-slaught of tourism. Come to Maine, the Medellin of the Northeast."

"What about Ray, Luke? Will the government renege on the departure?"

"Too late. It was their motion, after all, and the judge granted it.

C'est la guerre. But what a world! Ruiz and those thugs on one side, the DEA and the U.S. Attorney on the other, and a bunch of old hippie pot heads squeezed in the middle. `Everybody must get stoned!' Remember that? Well, it's worth your life these days. We might as well be living in Indonesia."

At that juncture in the conversation, we all lit up cigarettes. They can't bust you for that. Not yet.

ᴥ ᴥ ᴥ

We scarfed down some chili at Shoulders and then went to my house to scheme. I wasn't as optimistic as Luke about the grand jury, and I wouldn't put a coffee to go on Alzola getting charged with anything, not even kidnapping. He had a sharp lawyer who had kept him clean for years. Sharp lawyers can always find something wrong with a search warrant, because usually there is something wrong with it. Alzola probably could come up with a water-tight alibi for Saturday night and wind up filing a complaint against me for assault.

Over my dead body.

By the time we pulled into my driveway, I had turned into a raging P.I. from Hell.

I had to place Alzola in Peter Lawrence's apartment. I had to do it. Somebody must have seen somebody go into that apartment house Saturday night. José Ruiz had to have walked in, if no one else did.

Wilson made herself at home, which for her means she made herself a drink, kicked off her shoes and curled up in front of the TV. "My brain needs a rest," she said. "I have to plug in for a while." So what was she watching? Something on PBS about astrophysics and the phenomenon of black holes.

Meanwhile I called the tenants on Bennett Street. The Monahans on the first floor were elderly people who went to bed religiously at nine (I had caught them in the nick of time), got up at six and would be very happy to see us after their breakfast. Wilson volunteered for that. She loves old people, especially gabbers, says they remind her that there's life after sixty-five. (We are gradually moving our threshold forward. I remember when there wasn't supposed to be life after thirty.)

The second floor tenant, on the other hand, was less than enthusiastic about talking to me. Maybe he went to bed early, too, and I had just roused him from a REM cycle. Or maybe he was just slow.

"You're working for Peter Lawrence?" (Which I translated as, "You scumbag, how could you work for that slime?")

"For his attorney, to be precise."

There was a pause, as though he had nodded off on me. Then, "Mind if I check it out with Peter first?"

"Not at all," I said, trying not to sound stunned. "Want his number?"

"Five, seven, three, two, eight... Nope, I got his number. Call me back tomorrow, OK?"

Just to test a theory, I called three other names on Gareth's witness list. Each one of them wanted to run it by Peter first. This had never happened to me before.

"Hmm," Wilson said when I told her.

"Hmm, what?"

"Just 'hmm' for now. Maybe the Feds have been after him."

"After Peter? For what?"

"He has a friend from El Salvador, darling. What does that imply? What can you infer?"

There is something very massive, very dense, and very small ticking and purring inside M87: a black hole is implicated. Even if a black hole is invisible from the outside, its gravitational presence can be palpable.

"That he's a friendly sort of guy?"

If on an interstellar voyage you are not paying attention, you can find yourself drawn in...

"Could you turn that down a little?" She did, but the picture was still on. The cosmos as a whole in living color can divert your mind from details like where is El Salvador and what difference does it make if you have a friend who lives there.

"Remember that FBI flap a year or so ago? They had this massive surveillance and infiltration operation going on against CISPES, which stands for, let me think, Committee in Solidarity with the People of El Salvador. They were bugging phones and following people and breaking into offices, all very cloak and dagger and all totally illegal. Because CISPES was not in fact trying to overthrow the United States Government or any other government. They were collecting money to help the popular movement in Salvador and lobbying against military aid to the Salvadoran government and writing letters to get people out of jail down there. Pretty tame stuff. But the FBI had dreamt up this plot. You'd think they were all smoking crack themselves. It's the ultimate right-wing, drug-induced, paranoid fantasy: the poor and oppressed really are taking over the world! The meek really will inherit the earth! Tomorrow! Oh, my God, call out the Marines!... Can I turn the volume up again?"

"No. What does this have to do with Peter?"

"He's planning to take over the world, Jo. The faggots and the Indians and the Commies... Do you know in the Milky Way alone there are four hundred billion stars?"

"So the FBI came around asking questions about Peter because he's involved in CISPES...let's just say."

"Let's. And so his friends are wary and suspicious. Which is just how you want your friends to be when strange people come nosing around asking questions."

"Hmm," I said. "Or maybe he just supplies them all with pot and they're nervous."

"That too. I believe the FBI got its knuckles rapped over the CISPES thing. But there's nobody around gonna wrap the knuckles of the DEA. Not in our lifetimes anyway."

I turned the volume up for her and curled up on the couch with a cup of tea and a notebook. Wilson was getting her mind blown by the awesomeness of stars and galaxies; I snuggled next to her and began jotting down notes about mayhem and murder.

Chapter 13

Jim Devine met me at his door the following afternoon wearing day-glo orange shorts and a Hawaiian shirt. Well, what can you expect? June in Maine, and people go crazy with the tropical weather. Seventy-two degrees—a real heat wave.

He was one of those Vikings on thorazine, those big, fair, blue-eyed, bearded men with soft voices that are so laid back they could be in perpetual semi-hibernation. His girlfriend, Jen, was his physical duplicate, only a much smaller version. She was wearing a Guatemalan cotton shift, a serene blend of blues and greens. But soft-voiced and mellow as they were, they faced me like an armed camp.

We sat among jungle plants and ceramic stelae-shaped sculptures in their living room like three Arabs in an oasis bargaining over water rights. They had checked in with Peter and been informed that, yes, I was working for his lawyer, but what was it that I wanted from them exactly? They had been out of town that weekend. I said I knew that, I just wanted to ask them some questions about Peter himself and how they had met him and how long ago...

They exchanged a glance that was absurdly easy to read. What were they so scared about?

"Jen met Peter in art school," Jim said slowly, as though he had to excavate his brain to get at his memory. "So that's ten years ago. I met him through her, so that's five years."

"You consider him a friend? Not just an upstairs neighbor?"

"That's right. We're friends and neighbors."

"Do you know many of his other friends?"

"Peter has a lot of friends. We know some of them."

Like pulling teeth. I took a deep breath and tried a technique I disdain but use when necessary. Desperate times, as Will might say...

"You know that Peter is facing a murder indictment. It doesn't look too good for him, frankly. So if you want to help him, the best thing you can do is be frank with me, tell me everything, even the bad stuff, because that's what the prosecution will be after, all the shit they can dig up. We really need to know what's coming."

"So," Jen said, "you want us to give you some shit on Peter so you'll know what's coming? Well, we don't know any shit about Peter. He's a good friend."

"He sells pot. Did he ever sell pot to you?"

"Yeah," Jim said. "I've bought grass from him. So what? What does selling pot have to do with this murder trial?"

"The victim was a coke dealer. Did you know that?"

"Peter never did coke, never dealt coke. He's strictly a weed and mushroom man, and I can swear to that because I've been with him when he's turned down a line. Turned down coke deals, too. Man, Peter does not touch that shit."

"He doesn't even sell mushrooms," Jen said. "When he gets them he gives them away."

"Gives them away? Not very profitable, is it?"

"Peter believes mushrooms are too sacred to sell. Once a year he gets a shipment from California and we all go upcountry and eat them. It's a family ritual for us. Like Thanksgiving."

"You go up to his family's place?"

"Not to Old Town, no," Jim said. "Jen can't get her directions straight. She says upcountry, but it's really downeast, Washington County. He's got land up there."

"So when you say family, you really mean friends, right? Because to hear Peter tell it, the only family he's got is Jonathan."

"Well," Jim said, "I'd have to disagree with him on that."

"You know Jonathan?"

"Of course we know Jonathan."

"Like him?"

"Yeah."

"Is he a truthful person?"

"He's never lied to me," Jim said.

"I think," Jen said in her very soft voice, "that any gay man who comes out in this society should be presumed to be a truthful person. I've known Jonathan longer than Peter has and I will vouch for his honesty, if you need that."

"We might. Now about Peter himself. Is he ever violent? Like when he drinks maybe? Does he lose control?"

Jim sighed. "Peter Lawrence is the gentlest man I know. Straight or stoned. He doesn't drink alcohol by the way. Never has, to my knowledge. And as for losing control...ever watch a painter work?

What do you think a painter has to do to make the kind of work Peter makes up there? Have you seen it? He has to lose control. But is his work violent? No. Losing control and becoming violent are two entirely different things."

"He must get angry," I said. I felt like I was talking to the canonization committee.

"Sure he gets angry. I've seen him get pissed off. Read the newspaper with him sometime, he gets good and fucking angry. But he's non-violent and angry. `We are a gentle, angry people.' Know that song?"

"You must know his daughter, too."

"Zoe Neptune? Sure do."

"Neptune is her last name?"

"That's right."

"Her mother's name?"

"Actually, no. It's Peter's mother's family name. A good Penobscot name. I think it was the only surname they could agree on."

"I don't suppose you've ever seen him get angry at Zoe?"

"At Zoe? God, no. Those two are an item, big time. Mutual adoration. And he doesn't beat up on Jonathan either or throw the furniture around."

"He wasn't always so mellow. There was an incident on Indian Island..."

"Twelve, thirteen years ago. Yeah, I know about that. He was sixteen. A juvenile. They can't hit him with that."

"I see you've been giving this some thought."

"Of course we've given it some thought. But you can ask anybody who's studied Tae Kwon Do with Peter and they'll tell you about that incident, and you know why? Because Peter uses it, first meeting: this is a story of what can happen to you if you don't know how to defend yourself, and you don't know what you're doing. You can kill somebody in a fight, and then you have to live with it. I know because it happened to me...That's how he starts and you can bet your ass that after that people pay goddamn close attention."

"Does Peter sell grass from upstairs?"

"No. He delivers."

"So there aren't a lot of people going in and out?"

"No. It's his studio. He works up there."

"So, no company?"

"Not a lot, no. Sometimes people stop by to visit him, sure. ACT-UP met up there for a while. The Pledge of Resistance had a couple of meetings last year, I think it was. He puts people up when they come to town to visit, because he never sleeps there. So if I have friends visiting or other friends do, there's always a place for them to sleep. Last month there were two women staying up there. Friends of somebody he knew."

"He's the kind of person who'd do anything for you," Jen said.

The neighbors of serial killers have been known to express similar sentiments about them.

I made a great show of thumbing through my notes. "These women," I said, still thumbing, "One of them was named Michelle, wasn't she?"

"No," Jen said. "Alison and Janet, I think. Or Jeannette."

I kept thumbing. "Then who's Michelle? I know he mentioned somebody named Michelle."

"Zoe's mother," Jen said. "Peter's lover in a previous life. Her name is Michelle."

Well, knock me over with a feather. Peter had gone from one photographer to another the way some men go from blonde to blonde. He just had the gender wrong first time around. I'd have to take a little boat ride to Peaks one of these days and visit Zoe Neptune and her mom.

I was just about done. Done-in, too. It was actually pretty hot for June. I asked my last question, the big one: who might have killed José Ruiz in Peter's apartment? Come on, now, you've been giving this some thought, right? What do you think, guys? Who done it?

"Nobody we know. Nobody Peter knows, either. We think somebody brought these guys up to visit Peter, or just sent them..."

"So who would bring a couple of Colombian drug dealers up here to visit Peter?"

"Maybe whoever it was didn't know they were Colombian drug dealers. Maybe whoever it was just thought they were interesting guys."

"A friend or acquaintance of Peter's might just drop by with an interesting man for him?"

"Wait a minute! You're making it sound like procurement, or something... Look, let's get one thing straight, OK? Peter is not some..."

"OK, sorry," I said. (Just seeing if you're awake, Jim.) "But why would somebody just bring a stranger over here? For what purpose?"

"I told you. Because Peter is the kind of person who would help somebody out. Like if the guy was in transit."

"There's a refugee route through Maine," Jen said. "An underground railroad. For Central Americans en route to Canada. Peter knows the people who run it, and sometimes they ask him to shelter folks for a while. So if these guys are Latinos and get talking to a friend of Peter's and say they're on the run, need some help..."

"The friend might bring them over here. OK. But Ruiz wasn't a political refugee on the run."

"I'm just telling you that they could have come up looking for Peter. They could have. Then something happened between them."

"OK. Now when you say them you mean Ruiz and somebody else. Who do you imagine that somebody else could be?"

"Peter's got more friends in this town than the mayor. It could be anybody."

"A woman, maybe?"

"Sure a woman."

"A woman could have brought two interesting Latino men up here..."

"Sure. And left them here. And one of them killed the other one."

"You're thinking about this other man, Alzola?"

"Look. How many Latinos are there in Portland to begin with? All of a sudden one shows up dead and another one is busted for kidnapping and possession... Come on. Look, you need to find somebody who was home and awake Saturday night, right? Try the people in the blue house across the street, second floor. They're night owls. If anybody saw anything Saturday night, it'd be them."

"Are they friends of Peter's too?"

He smiled and shrugged. I dutifully took their names, but I knew I couldn't handle another one of these canonization interviews, not back to back. I wasn't even sure I could handle another one any time in the foreseeable future. It was just about Courage time and Courage was just what I needed.

I thanked them for their time and went looking for Will.

Chapter 14

"We got a face!" Wilson said, plopping a sheet of drawing paper down on my desk and looking triumphant. "Eureka, right?"

The face was oval and doe-eyed, pretty though a bit vacuous, sort of Miss Reingold pretty. Regular, normal, WASPy, pretty.

"Eureka, my ass. You didn't find this face. You made it up."

"Monica made it up. Russ the Bartender helped."

"Monica is supposed to be a composite sketch artist. What kind of composite do you get from one witness?"

"Well, shit," she said, and sat down. The amethyst crystal was sparkling away right under her nose. She put her hand on it to feel it or cover it up, I don't know which. "What rabid dog bit you this afternoon?"

"I don't know, Will. I just keep getting the feeling that everybody is lying."

"Everybody?"

"Yup. Everybody. Even Russ the Bartender. Probably he's in love with Peter Lawrence, too."

"Who else is in love with Peter Lawrence?"

"His downstairs neighbors. His across-the-street neighbors. His main squeeze, alias Mr. Alibi."

"And why are all these people lying again? Because Peter did kill José Ruiz, they all know it, and they're covering for him? Is that it?"

"No. No, I'm just losing it, that's all...OK, so what's the plan here? We take Miss America to all the straight bars, ask if anybody knows her and wait to see who kidnaps us?"

"Or we take it to DEA and see if they know her. Might save us a lot of time."

"Tell me you're not serious. I mean, this isn't even a real person's face."

"Russ says that's the lady. Russ saw her."

"Russ wants to blow Peter Lawrence so bad he can fucking taste it."

"Come on, sugar. I'm taking you to Shoulders for some libations. You need some fun in your life..."

❧ ❧ ❧

An hour later we were back on the topic again after a pleasant hiatus of beer ordering, beer drinking and a couple of dart games. The fun in my life; now it was business again.

"The question I have," I said, "the one big prominent question I have, is why whoever it was—Alzola, Michelle, whoever—why they picked Peter Lawrence's apartment. I mean, of all the apartments in all the towns in all the world, why off José Ruiz in his?"

"The gay angle. Has to be."

"Random choice. Any old gay man's apartment would do, but his won. And how did they even know about his existence?"

"What does Peter Lawrence have in common with José Ruiz? D-O-P-E. Now, where do we think Peter Lawrence got his grass from?"

"I don't know. I never thought to ask."

"Well, does he import it? Does he buy it from..."

"Downeast. He's got land downeast. I bet it's home grown."

"And where does Ray Boulanger deal from?"

"Downeast."

"Bingo."

"Downeast is a pretty big place, Will."

"And it's got mighty few people in it. This is a goddamn small state, distances notwithstanding. When does the grand jury meet?"

"Four weeks."

"Sure would be nice to have this all together by then, wouldn't it?"

"And then go on vacation."

"Where do you want to go?"

"Lisbon."

"OK. I'll make a deal with you. We get our man by Bastille Day, we catch the next plane to Lisbon."

"Or our woman," I said, thinking of the oval face of Michelle. *"Cherchez la femme*, remember?"

"She never touched that rock," Wilson said. "She was bait. Bait, pure and simple."

"But whose bait?"

"That's the question. You know what we need? We need food for thought. Let's go cook up some pasta."

"I thought it was fish. Brain food, that is."

"I have a can of clam sauce in the pantry. What d'ya say? Are we on?"

❧ ❧ ❧

The nice thing about pasta is that you can cook it in a state of total distraction. Eat it that way, too. You don't even have to think about chewing it. To my knowledge nobody has ever choked to death on macaroni.

As I expected, Wilson had drawn a blank with the Monahans. Heard all about Peter, of course. But of things that go bang in the night, zip. For old people, they slept like logs.

While Will talked, she rolled us a joint. While she rolled the joint, I put a salad together out of the green stuff buried in her refrigerator. Otherwise it would have been an entirely white meal, even the salad dressing was white. Low fat Ranch. I know Wilson, so I know that everything she buys is accidental. Low fat, high fat—these are not categories Wilson deals with. She bought salt-free V-8 by mistake once and gagged on it over breakfast. "What the fuck! They're trying to poison us!" I've seen her salt salt-free peanuts, but it's useless to remind her to read the labels. She shops by color.

"I wonder," she said handing me the joint, "if this is Laurentian grass."

"Laurentian? Is that a new part of Mexico? Or are they importing it from Canada?"

"From the native soil of Maine, natural and hearty as the potato, Laurentian marijuana, brought to you from the private stock of M. Peter Lawrence."

"Ah. Could be I guess. Who do you buy from?"

"My friend Danielle. And you?"

"My next door neighbor."

"It's a friendly little underground, isn't it? As American as apple pie and the free enterprise system, rooted in individual initiative and based on mutual trust. What will we do when all our dealers are in the joint?"

"We'll be right in there with them. Zero tolerance, my dear, means even a simple joint will one day condemn you to penal servitude."

"Did you say penile servitude?" She slurped up some spaghetti. "But such a nice little herb. Makes you appreciate the cosmos a little more, brings you directly to your senses, expands the corridors..."

"Stop. You sound like a NORML commercial."

"Well, they should repeal the marijuana laws, goddamnit. Cannabis, drug of the century. Cures glaucoma. Relieves pain. Settles the stomach. Plus you can use every part of it, make clothes out of the fiber, rope. Hemp rope, remember that? Paper. Did you know the Declaration of Independence was written on paper made of hemp? Hemp has no natural enemies except man. No boll weevils chomp on little hemp plants. We could save the forests by making paper out of hemp again. Instead we're burning it, poisoning it—plant genocide. And you want to know something else? Marijuana is Maine's number one cash crop. Yes. I read it in the post office. The plant's on a Wanted Poster hanging in the post office, can you believe it? And the poster says, Did you know Maine's #1 crop is ILLEGAL? Now what the fuck does that tell you?"

"It tells me—aside from the fact that you went to the post office recently—that if home grown is the #1 cash crop in this state, then either people have given up eating potatoes or there is no Mexican weed coming into this country anymore. Remember Michoacan? Remember Jamaican red? Acapulco gold? God, and what are we stuck with now? Lousy Maine home grown."

"Listen to me. What did Luke say yesterday at the bar? The cartel on one side, the DEA on the other, pot heads squeezed in between. And not just the smokers—the growers. Maine's number one cash crop, Wilder. You know how much it's worth? I did a little checking this afternoon. The Maine marijuana crop is worth approximately a quarter of a billion dollars. Two hundred and fifty million dollars. The runner up, potatoes, rings in at one hundred and sixty million. And lobster is a paltry fifty million. This is a poor state. A very poor state. And we're talking big money."

I forgot I was holding a joint and inhaled it like it was a cigarette. By the time I stopped coughing, Wilson had taken one of those mental quantum leaps that hemp seems to encourage. From cash crops to...

"Do you still have the witness list from the Boulanger case?"

"In the office."

"Let's go get it."

"Now? What about supper?"

"Well, stop talking so much and eat. We need that list."

I remembered I was supposed to be eating and dug in. Wilson, however, kept talking.

"See, I was a cop once upon a time, as you may recall, and my vestigial cop sense tells me that Alzola didn't kill Ruiz, not there, not like that. Luke is right. They're not that clever to play the gay angle. It's too baroque for the hoodlum brain. Only people like us would think of something like that. Anyway the Feds want Alzola bad, so let's leave him to them and then figure the other options just in case they blow it. Which I'll lay odds they do. You don't want Peter taking this rap, do you? Mrs. Monahan is praying for him. To St. Jude. So let's make her a happy woman and do the impossible. St. Jude can take the credit."

"Good," I said, too stoned now to be following everything. Baroque, huh? Was Wilson taking art history classes on the Q.T.?

"OK. So let's re-examine motive. Say it's not the cartel offing Ruiz to protect its interests. Say it's the Maine pot growers offing Ruiz to protect *its* interests. Tra-la, my darlin'! New scenario. Then first, we're looking for a woman. Michelle probably isn't her real name. Second, we're looking for property owners who may be growing Maine's number one cash crop. Third, we have to get from Luke the names of other defendants in cocaine busts and talk to them."

"Why?"

"Why? Because somebody killed José Ruiz in Peter Lawrence's apartment. That much we know. He didn't hit himself on the head. So far we have three possibilities: Peter Lawrence killed him; Enrique Alzola or his agent killed him; Michelle or a confederate of hers killed him. If we drop Peter as a suspect, we run head on into the problem of his apartment. Now if Michelle, working either for Alzola or for some other party, brought José to Peter's apartment..."

"Then she had to know Peter."

"Right. If José brought *her* there..."

"Then *he* had to know Peter."

"So we have to find the place where Peter interfaces with either Alzola or Michelle and company."

"What do you think about Jim Devine's theory that Michelle picked the two of them up and brought them to Peter's and left them there..."

"I think it's bullshit."

"You're happier thinking Michelle was bait for the pot growers?"

"What's another alternative? We need something to work on. We need a useful fiction."

"OK. Here's one. José is cruising town. This woman picks him up. He's flashing money. She excuses herself, calls her cohort, says, 'I've got a big one on the hook.' Cohort says, 'Bring him to Peter's place.' She brings him telling him it's her place. Cohort kills him and they split the dough. Murder and robbery."

"That's nice, Wilder. I like that. Turning tricks in a painter's studio—very Left Bank, isn't it? Of course, it doesn't explain why Alzola grabbed you off the street."

"And it doesn't explain the sheet over the painting...This is excellent clam sauce by the way."

"Thanks. I picked it off the shelf myself...What sheet?"

"If I were a homicide detective, which I'm not, I'd have that sheet sent to the forensic lab."

"What sheet? What sheet? What are you talking about?"

"There is a sheet over one of Peter's paintings. I told you. Now explain that with a useful fiction. Or maybe it was just arbitrary. Maybe that day he looked at his painting and thought, God, that sucks. I can't stand looking at it... So he covered it up with a sheet. I mean, Will, the problem is there is no explanation for everything because half of everything is completely arbitrary and irrational. Half of it is chaos and the other half only makes sense if you're inside it. The rationale for most of what we do is completely private. It doesn't have to do with reason; it has to do with affinity, feelings, desires, attractions..."

I stopped then because I couldn't recall the beginning of the sentence. I had no idea where I had started out to get to "desires and attractions." These things happen when you're stoned.

"Like for example," I remembered the sheet. "Take the sheet. What if I say to you, I know Peter Lawrence was involved in that murder because he covered his painting up with a sheet."

"Oh, well," Wilson said. "We don't have to go anywhere tonight. The list will keep. I'm going to have another beer. Just keep talking."

"Oh, good," I said, though in fact I had forgotten that we were supposed to go anywhere. She left the room and came back with two cold beers and said, "Go on."

"What was I saying?"

"Peter is guilty because of a sheet."

"Right. He covered a wet painting with a sheet."

"Or somebody else did."

"Why would somebody else cover it?"

"Why would he cover it?"

"To protect it."

"From what?"

"Blood. Bad vibes. The sight of a murder being done...He's a weird guy, Will. Remember that painting by Gauguin, *The Spirit of the Dead Watching*?"

"I don't know, Jo. It's pretty far fetched."

"Of course it is. It's irrational. But that's just what I'm getting at. No useful fiction is going to explain that sheet."

"OK. Here's one. Here's a useful fiction for you. The pot growers of Maine are caught between the devil and the deep blue sea, the Colombian Mafia on one side, the Feds on the other. They decide they can handle one but not both, so they take on the Mafia. Turf war. José Ruiz was moving in on their turf, so they killed him."

"I like that."

"Thought you would."

"I'm rooting for Estonia, too. Besides this doesn't get Peter off the hook."

"Peter didn't have to be in on it. They just used his place."

"I really dislike friends who drop in unannounced and leave messes behind them."

"Obviously they weren't his friends."

"Obviously not."

Wilson pushed away her glass of wine, since she had switched to beer. I hadn't touched mine either, but the color was gorgeous.

"I wonder what he named those paintings."

"Who?"

"Peter. Or if he's one of those painters who call everything *Untitled #22* or *Linear Development #4*. Me, I'd name them *The Lovers* or *What Love Looks Like in the Light* or..."

"But you think he killed Ruiz? I mean, that's your gut feeling...Wilder? Come back to me."

I was trying to remember those long, lean shapes, so male, nothing feminine about them, not if you think of shapes in terms of gender, or vice versa.

"But why would he?" Thinking aloud, something you only have the luxury of doing in the presence of someone who knows you very well. "You'd have to be a lunatic to kill someone like that, in your own house, and wait hours to call it in, not even try to dump the body anywhere..."

"Unless he's shielding someone."

"God, Will, this is America in the twilight years of the twentieth century. Nobody *shields* anybody anymore..."

She got up and went to her briefcase. When she came back she was holding the sketch of Michelle.

"That couldn't be a man in drag, could it? You said Jonathan Hall was blonde and cute. Add some eyeliner, some mascara, some blush..."

"Jonathan a transvestite? He picks up Ruiz, it gets nasty, he hits him with the amethyst..." I could almost see it. "It would explain so much."

"It's a pretty terrific working fiction, isn't it? Or another version: beautiful but faithless drag queen, jealous lover, naked Colombian caught in *flagrante delicto*... I could get into it."

"It's been done," I said. But, of course, so what? That story was old, all the stories were old. That didn't keep people from believing them, acting them out, living by them, dying for them. The story may have been around for eons, but when it's happening to you it's happening for the first time. The first love, the first betrayal, the first homicidal rage, the first murder.

I kept staring at the sketch, and the more I stared at it the more like Jonathan Hall Michelle became.

"Jo," Wilson said, and she put her arm around me. "It's very far fetched. Russ is a bartender, after all, so he's practically an expert on gender and he'd have noticed if Michelle was in drag. But you met him, not me. What do you think?"

At that point and simultaneously, I thought two things. One was that I had been projecting every true love fantasy I had onto Peter Lawrence and Jonathan Hall when I might have looked right across the dinner table for it, and the second was that I was going to find out who killed José Ruiz if only because Wilson was in on it with me and she was like one of those little pit bulls who grab hold and never let go. So we'd find the killer. But whether I'd be happy with what we found, that was another question altogether.

Chapter 15

Like two good monomaniacs Wilson and I spent the next morning—a sunny Saturday morning no less—on the phone. I kept telling myself it was too chilly to be a good beach day, though lying in the sand, even under a blanket, had its appeal. I hadn't been to the beach all year. I was waiting for the season to start, which in Maine can mean staying pale as death until August.

I found Boulanger's witness list and called them one by one. One by one they turned me down. Albert Greer was polite but non-committal. He didn't want to talk anymore now that Ray was cooperating. Didn't see the point. And what if the government reneged on the deal? I asked. "When they renege on the deal," Albert said, "then call me."

George Smith was neither polite nor non-committal. He would not talk to me. Period.

But I had spent an afternoon with George Smith up near Jonesport. It had been the kind of day you think of when you think of the Outer Hebrides, if you should ever happen to think of the Outer Hebrides. Cold, wet, dismal, haunting, mysterious, the sea raging against the rocks, the land mist-enshrouded, wind and rain slapping against the windows of his house which was set like a lighthouse right on the rocks, while fog horns bayed and lobster boats bobbed in the harbor. The air was thick with the smell of the sea, of fish and tobacco and wet wool and wood smoke. We had started off drinking coffee, laced the dregs with hard liquor, ended up drinking out of the bottle. He told me stories of bringing in thousands of pounds of weed the way fishermen might tell of bringing in thousands of pounds of herring. The same storms at sea, the same fifty foot waves, but also other dangers: the Coast Guard, pirates. Pirates! Like stories from the pen of Robert Louis Stevenson, and he told them with the dry uninflected accent of a downeaster, an accent I'm told is as close to pure Elizabethan speech as we're likely to find anywhere on the planet. He had trusted me with those stories and I had trusted him to tell me the truth. But he hadn't told me the truth, and now he was cutting bait on me. I might not have any right to be pissed off, but I was.

"Why didn't you tell me the Colombians had threatened Ray's family? Don't tell me you didn't know! I know you did know. And that bastard kidnapped me, George. I could be dead now."

There was an elongated pause on the other end.

"Are you still there, George?"

"Ayuh," he said.

"Why didn't you tell me?"

"Ray didn't want it to get around. His wife and kids—he was scared for them. But it's over now."

"No, it's not over. Ruiz is dead, yes. But his boss, Alzola, is still alive and well."

"That one's got nothin' to do with us."

I looked across the desk to Wilson who was listening in on the other phone. She gave me the nod: play it out. That's what useful fictions are for. I took a long breath, touched the amethyst with my finger for luck (luck?) and said, "And what happens when he finds out Boulanger set up his buddy, George?"

"Who says that?" he asked, slow and deliberate.

"I do." Wilson shook her head vigorously and scribbled a note. NOT YOU. THE FEDS. But at the same time George laughed.

"Oh, babe," he said, "you've been smokin' too much reefer. Ray had nothin' to do with Ruiz. Nothin' whatever. That bastard was killed getting his ass fucked and you know it as well as me. I'm no homo hater, Johannah, but facts are facts."

What a jury pool Peter Lawrence was going to have. Polluted as a pond of acid rain.

ૐ ૐ ૐ

We had grounded out with Boulanger's people. Wilson wanted to start right in with Luke's old cocaine clientele, but I for one wasn't going to drive to the state prison to interview cocaine dealers on a beautiful Saturday afternoon. There are limits to my dedication, even to truth, justice and the American way.

What was left for us was to find Michelle. *Cherchez la femme.* According to Wilson's useful fiction she'd be up in the cannabis fields or blueberry barrens of Washington County; according to mine she'd be right down here among the lowlife of Portland. If our Michelle was a lady of ill repute, the Portland vice cops would know her. This is a pretty small town.

We spent the rest of the day in the Public Safety Building trying to find Michelle among the mug shots of hookers, masseuses, exotic dancers and transvestite hustlers. The vice cops were their usual sleazy selves. One of them told us what he thought was a hysterical story about a john IDing his contacts in exchange for immunity, picking out his regular girls from the photo line-up. One of his regulars turned out to be a kid named Joey Martin who liked to hustle in drag. The cop chortled. And guess what? (This is the punch-line.) The dumb john never knew the difference!

Wilson and I agreed it was the funniest thing since knock-knock jokes. Of course we didn't see anybody male or female who looked like Michelle.

We emerged from the Bastille just as the foghorns began bleating like lost sheep. Within minutes the cold, clammy sea fog would start drifting in, creeping over the low brick buildings of the Old Port. Already the thick bank was visible on Munjoy Hill. Or rather, the fog was visible; the Hill itself had disappeared.

"Another night inside a cloud," Wilson sighed.

"The cloud of unknowing."

"You can say that again. Let's go have a healthy shot of scotch so we can face it all with equanimity. Next stop the escort services."

"The massage parlors."

"The bookstore. I want to buy a guidebook to Portugal."

"You're such an optimist."

"Hey, we can always look at the pictures."

I love the woman, though she will turn me into a crazy old lady before my time.

ða ða ða

Over Glenlivet we read to each other from the guidebook and studied all the photographs. Portugal seemed lovely, but as remote from our current location as two places could be. For one thing, it looked like it was always sunny in Portugal. Here, even though it was June, people were coming into the bar in droves just to get warm.

"Let me see your calendar so I can count the days." Unlike myself, Wilson does not hold to the principle that calendars belong on walls. She carries hers around in a leather binding, and more often that not my appointments appear on it as well as her own. She is obsessional and doesn't trust my memory.

"What's the date today?"

She groaned and pointed it out to me. "Well, good for you, Jo. You're in the right month. Hey, this is Gay Pride weekend."

"That explains where Solange is. Marching with Dykes on Bikes." And then my eye fell on the previous Sunday's designation. Like being slapped in the face.

"Oh my God," I said.

"What?"

"Last Sunday was Father's Day."

"Shit. I forgot to send my dad a card."

"Wilson, last Sunday was Father's day."

"I heard you the first time."

"Peter Lawrence is a father."

"So?"

"So, children spend Father's Day with their fathers. Peter's daughter wasn't with him last weekend."

"Oh, Jesus, Jo. I thought it was something important! Maybe he doesn't keep in touch with her."

"He does."

"Maybe the mother doesn't let her daughter stay overnight. After all, he's a gay man living with his lover. Maybe she was planning to see him on Sunday but on Sunday he was in the county jail."

"Maybe."

"What are you getting at?"

"Only that if he was planning on killing someone on Saturday night, he wouldn't be having his daughter come for the weekend."

Wilson plucked a cigarette out of my pack and twirled it between her fingers. "And why would he be planning to kill someone on Saturday night again?"

"Because he's jealous. Because Jonathan is seeing another man. Because Jonathan is Michelle. It explains so much, Will. It gives us a motive. And you saw that photo of Joey Martin. He's just a punk kid with a little Mary Kay. Imagine if you really knew how to use make-up, imagine..."

"OK, it explains a lot. So does Original Sin. Doesn't mean it's true. It's a useful fiction. The world is filled to the gills with useful fictions. When they outlive their usefulness, then you see what crap they are."

"Well," I said, downing the remainder of my shot, "I'm ready."

"For what?"

"It's Family Festival week down at the Oaks. I want you to take me on all the kiddie rides and win me a big stuffed bear."

Wilson shook her head at me. "You're getting too involved. Lighten up, Jo. It's not like he's your best friend or anything."

"No. But when you decide to brain someone, will you be kind enough to dispose of the body in a public place?"

"I promise you. Right smack dab in front of City Hall."

"Thank you."

"You're welcome... Are you serious about the bear?"

"Dead serious. I've never won a big stuffed bear in my life, but if you win one for me, I'll win one for you. Or go broke in the attempt. What d'ya say?"

"We might have a crack at it at the shooting booths. OK, I'm game. Anyway we need something to take our minds off work."

I just grinned at her. The only thing that would take Will's mind off work was decapitation. I was easier. I figured a few rides on the roller coaster would erase Peter Lawrence from my mind for at least the rest of the night.

Chapter 16

The Deering Oaks Family Festival is a strange brew, the urban version of a county fair, all the folderol without the 4-H, or as Wilson put it the first time we came, So where's the beef? The nearest thing to wild animals are the dazed, lugubrious ponies that devote their lives to carrying kids around on their backs in a circular enclosure, vying for customers against the louder and glitzier mechanical rides, the helicopter, boat, firetruck and rocket ship merry-go-rounds that not only go around but lift off the ground as well.

These kiddie rides are on the high ground in the wooded section of the park. Below them on the flat playing fields are the grown-up versions: the big ferris wheel, the haunted house and the special treats for virulent masochists—the Zipper and the Salt 'n Pepper, on which you are locked in a cage, lifted off the ground, flipped upside down and spun, all while hurtling through space at a high rate of speed. The roar of the Zipper and the screams of those riding on it can be heard all over the park, as though some massive open-air torture and execution were being held for the amusement of the citizens of our fair city. Also on the playing fields and along the park road are hucksters selling everything from plastic pirate swords to psychedelic posters and heavily tattooed shills luring people toward the wheels of fortune, the duck shoots, the dart games, the betting booths and all those guess-your-weight, guess-your-age wizards and the Everybody Wins, Four Chances for a Buck booths that people flock to like lemmings. Dispersed through the bedlam are food stands decorated in pulsating yellow neon selling corn on the cob, popcorn, cotton candy, fried dough, fries in vinegar and pizza. At night the whole monstrous thing turns lurid, lit in throbbing red and orange neon, filled with half-dressed, half-drunken people and besieged by mosquitoes.

And how could I even mention the Festival without describing the ever-popular helicopter rides which make living in the city during those marvelous Festival days seem like living in a war zone, the drone of the copters circling overhead at fifteen minute intervals, the way they hover menacingly, the mad desire that rises inside you to get yourself a high-powered rifle and shoot them down.

But in the proper frame of mind, the Festival has a certain momentary charm. Something about the energy of the hucksters ("Two shots for a buck! Win a prize! Try your luck! Test your skill!"), the shrieks of agonized pleasure emanating from the Zipper, the smell of popcorn, the crush of bodies, the tension at the betting booths, the darkness hovering at the edge of the lights...

And the darkness isn't confined to the fringes. Under the trees by the kiddie rides, in the spaces between stall and booth, the darkness creeps in. Children, separated from their parents, get lost in these spaces. Drug deals go down. Bodies get bought. The air throbs and pulses with light, music, voices, screams. If you let go of your companion, you lose her instantly in the crowd. People wander, lost or searching, in those dark spaces. Creepy, those shadows amid so much light.

ટ્ટ ટ્ટ ટ્ટ

We were donating money to the bottle fund ("Get the dime in the bottle! Test your skill! Win a prize!") when I glanced up and saw Solange LaBelle tossing her dimes away with equal abandon. I waited until Wilson finished her throw and then grabbed her arm. "Look!"

"Out of town, my ass," she said and started moving. But the booth was big, rectilinear, and Solange was on the other side of it. By the time we fought our way over, she had moved on. We saw her pause at the goldfish ("Get a ball in the bowl! Win the fish! Three balls for a buck!") and then we lost visual contact.

"Will, wait!" I yelled, but Wilson was part hound and had picked up the scent.

"Circle around!" she yelled back. "If we don't collide, meet me back here in fifteen minutes."

But, I thought loudly, What do I do if I collide with LaBelle?

Our telepathic skills aren't finely tuned. I didn't get a response.

But I am nothing if not obedient, and I circled around the goldfish, noticing how many little kids were carrying plastic baggies of water and goldfish. I'd have to try this one; maybe I could go home with something after all.

Outside the magic circle of music and neon lights, it was getting dark and the air was chilly and dank. The fog bank that had settled over the Hill had spread into the Cove and was creeping into the Oaks. Wisps of cloud hung over the top of the ferris wheel whose skeleton was now outlined in orange neon. Wisps of cloud even hung over the crowd, changing the way sounds resonated, making everything seem closer. In the larger darkness of the park, the street lamps did not so much illuminate space as glow like huge fireflies in the mist. Parents were gathering up children, teenagers were moving in packs, gathering in their strays. And through all this the willing victims on the Zipper still screamed, the music still played, the potatoes still sizzled in hot grease, and Solange LaBelle's half-shaven bleached blonde head and black leather jacket flittered for a second in front of my eyes not three booths away.

Damn, I said, and strode toward her.

But something else got in the way. It was a very long, straight, black ponytail hanging down the back of a rather tall man who was walking away from me in the direction of the kiddie rides. Next to the man was a little girl. She was dancing along beside him, holding a plastic bag filled with water and a goldfish in her right hand. Her left hand was being held quite securely by another adult, whose shape was somewhat disguised by a bulky sweater but who most assuredly had blonde hair.

I could have been wrong, of course, but from behind it sure looked to me like a version of the new nuclear family: Peter Lawrence, Zoe Neptune and Jonathan Hall. But was that tall man really Peter Lawrence? Would Jonathan Hall be carrying a leather shoulder purse? Had his hair been that fluffy? (Nothing a hair dryer couldn't do, of course.) And was that a man's walk? And where was Wilson?

I hesitated and Solange disappeared behind a ticket line. But to my joy Wilson was coming in on an angle, her hair all frizzed up from the dampness, her hands shoved into her pockets. She had Solange in her sights. With a clear conscience I detoured and followed the trio in the other direction.

ea ea ea

The path up to the kiddie rides was lined with food stands. There was a fight starting in front of one of them, two overweight street toughs pushing each other around. A clutch of hairspray warriors in skin tight jeans and halter tops watched cool-eyed from the side-lines smoking Marlboros. The family segment of the Family Festival had come to an end.

It was like snapping awake out of a dream and seeing where you really were. A group of teenagers were passing a can of beer around while a few feet away grown men whose appearance was living testimony to the moral and physical degeneration of the white race were looking at passing women in a way that made me want to gouge their eyes out. Soggy twelve year olds who should have been home getting tucked in for the night were smoking cigarettes and eyeing the hookers who had appeared miraculously from out of the darkness of the fringe. Candy wrappers, popcorn containers, sticky cotton candy cones and soda cans were overflowing from a trash can. Mixed with the trash I noticed a dead goldfish on the ground.

I had lost the trio in the crowd, but I knew where they were headed. I abandoned the path and tried to make my way up the grassy incline toward the kiddie rides. I thought it would be a short cut. Dumb move. I ran into ticket lines. I ran into food lines. I ran into electric cable lines. I found myself going in circles, blocked from going upward by crates of soda bottles and the backsides of game booths. Shit.

Meanwhile security had rushed to the scene below and dispersed the hoodlum element. I skidded back down to the path and began pushing my way up, past the slow but steady exodus of baby strollers and yuppie couples. I was determined to find Peter, if it was Peter, but I had lost precious time. I felt like I was clawing my way through these molasses slow people, like I was a kid myself racing to get to the rocket ships and the firetrucks for my last ride of the night.

Back on flat ground at last, I went from ride to ride, peering at the faces of adults watching kids go 'round and 'round. Such total absorption was unnerving, like watching the hypnotized. Every so often somebody woke up enough to slap a bare arm or bare leg. The 'skeets were out in full force.

Peter wasn't at the firetrucks or the tanks or the submarines. The last ride, way at the end, was the big carousel with its beautiful life-size painted horses, three deep, some decked in garlands of roses, some rearing, some prancing, some frozen in mid-stride, gray ones, white ones and black, their faces painted with expression, intelligence and passion in the eyes, all going up and down to the music of a Viennese waltz with little kids clutching onto their necks.

The moisture in the air was turning into drizzle, but the carousel was covered and brightly lit with white lights so only the waiting adults noticed the rain. They moved closer to their partners, buttoned up their coats.

All around the carousel, hidden in the branches of the old elms and maple trees, were stadium lights; this section of the park, like no other, was completely illuminated. And in the strange, abnormal brightness surrounding the carousel, I saw them.

Peter Lawrence had taken his jacket off and put it around the shoulders of the small blonde person standing beside him. It had a hood, and the small blonde person had pulled the hood up. Peter was holding the goldfish and as the carousel made its turn he waved, and a child on the black horse with the red rose garland over its shoulders waved back.

In Europe men wear jackets over their shoulders, but it is a rare sight in Portland. In Europe men carry leather shoulder bags, too. Of course, Jonathan Hall could carry a leather purse if he wanted. Walking beside a martial arts black belt, Jonathan Hall could probably get away with wearing high heels and a dress.

The simplest thing to do would be to go over and say hello. We did know each other after all. But I hesitated again. The drizzle was turning into a steady rain and the ride had ended. I watched Zoe jump off the platform and run toward her father. Passing the goldfish to his companion, he caught the child in both hands as she leapt at him and lifted her into the air. She leaned over and threw her arms around the small blonde person who kissed her cheek.

Peter turned and started walking toward the street carrying his daughter on his shoulders. He was holding his companion's hand.

I took three giant steps forward and stopped. I stood in the rain and watched them leave the park. I told myself it would be an invasion of his privacy to speak with Peter now. I told myself I had no business interfering with his time with his daughter. I told myself it was raining too hard.

Right, Johannah.

When Peter's companion kissed Zoe, the hood had fallen back enough so that in the starkness of the stadium lights I could get a glimpse of a face. Not of an entire face, but of lips. They were accentuated lips, or as the pulp novels say, painted lips. They were lips that properly, "normally," belonged on a woman's face.

But who else would Peter Lawrence hold hands with in public but his lover, Jonathan Hall?

Chapter 17

Wilson's call woke me at the ungodly hour of 10 AM.

"Sorry I deeked you last night," she said cheerily. "You didn't wait too long, I hope."

I had waited all of ten minutes for Wilson in the rain by the drowning goldfish, but she had deeked me, that was a fact, and hadn't even bothered to call me later to see if I made it home. I could still be waiting there for all she knew.

"No," I said. "Not too long. And Solange?"

"Yeah," she said. "Well I'll tell you when I see you."

"But did you catch up with her?"

"Yes."

"And you talked to her?"

"Negotiations are still in progress. We're making headway, I think."

"Oh," I said. "How nice for both of you. Guess I'll see you tomorrow then." And I hung up. I'd no sooner put the phone down than it rang again.

"All right," I said into the receiver. "I'm sorry. It's just that I'm not awake, I'm intensely irritated at the world and then you call sounding like the cat that swallowed the canary..."

There was a slight throat clearing at the other end and a voice that was clearly male said, "Johannah? This is Luke Neville. Sorry. I guess Sunday morning isn't the best time to call."

"Oh, hi, Luke. No, it's a perfect time. I just always answer my phone like I'm deranged. Discourages the perverts. What's up?"

What was up was that Luke was going to be in trial for the next few days and wanted to give us some information on the Bridgton murder in case we had any spare time and wanted to get going on it. "Before everybody forgets everything," as he put it. I dutifully copied down names and phone numbers, directions like: Three quarters of a mile past the house with the yard full of cannibalized wrecks there's a stand of old growth pine. First dirt road on the left, to the third fork. At the boulder hang a hard left...

How do the Feds ever bust anybody out there? How do they find anybody out there?

"Now listen, Johannah," he said. "No heroics on this one, OK? Remember that whoever killed Bobby Freer is either a lunatic or a very nasty customer. Keep a low profile, take no chances. Maybe you'd even want them to come into town for this."

I reminded Luke that it was preferable to interview people on their own turf where they felt comfortable and we could check out their taste in home furnishings.

"Just be cool then. I know, you were born cool, right?"

I was born cool all right, so cool that I was going to turn this whole mess over to Wilson. I had a long list of restless clients who were waiting for me to find their current or ex-spouses, their run-away children or their lost pets. And I had to find a woman named Michelle. Though I was 99% sure that I already knew who she was. I was 99% sure that I had seen Peter Lawrence holding hands with her in the Oaks.

Unless Peter was two-timing Jonathan with a small blonde woman. After all, anything is possible.

ò ò ò

My social life had been on hold for weeks, thanks to the search for Solange. I had missed two good movies, passed up the chance to go to a friend's camp for a weekend and turned down dinner invitations from both my next door neighbor and my Greek reading group with whom I am bonded as only men and women can be bonded who have spent a year of their lives decoding Homeric Greek together. I thought I wanted to go out with people that night, but the more I considered it, the less appealing the prospect was. I was despondent and didn't feel like subjecting any one of my friends to such overt negativity. Instead as soon as it got dark, I went out for a walk.

"Walking the Boulevard" is a thing to do in this town. The Boulevard is Baxter Boulevard, which winds around the littoral of Back Cove. It's about a three mile walk from west to east along a dirt path with the cove on your right and the boulevard with its expensive houses set on a slight rise on your left. The path is used by runners, bicyclists and power walkers as well as people just out for a stroll. From this path downtown Portland across the cove can look like a real city or like a fairy tale city, depending on the light; in either case, it looks pretty good.

You see how the peninsula curves, you see the Hill rise majestically with the Observatory at its peak, and then you see where the cove empties into the bay and Tukey's Bridge, which connects the peninsula to the mainland, and the B and M bean factory on the other side. The cove itself is a haven for seabirds, who nest in the marshes at its banks, and for harbor seals who sun themselves on its rocks at low tide. To me the Boulevard is a perfect example of ecological harmony: cars and bikes and human beings and herons and seals and cats and dogs and gulls and little fishies in the water, all co-existing in one place at one time. And I have never once seen a cop on the Boulevard except passing in a squad car, never once seen a foot patrolman walking a Baxter Boulevard beat.

That night I must have been in a state of heightened awareness, brought on by solitude or by the tiny bit of pot I smoked before I left the house or by some sort of yearning I couldn't identify, desire without a name. Or maybe it was the result of turning off that part of my brain that fiddled with problems like hands with a Rubik's cube, turning them this way and that way, trying to get the pieces to fit. Like Greek grammar, the puzzle was a code that had to be broken. But it wasn't fun anymore, this particular puzzle. It was shaking down to be something that wasn't fun.

So I turned my brain off and let my senses loose on the world. Walking the Boulevard, walking meditation. Walking there and being nowhere else. Being where you are.

First I noticed the sounds. I kept thinking a bike was coming up behind me; it was only the ticking song of the crickets. There was a high-pitched twittering in the marsh grasses; it was the nestlings. From farther out on the glassy smooth water, the sounds of wild ducks and geese, conversing. A black cat came up out of the marsh grass and cocked his tail and came over to say hello. Then I looked across the water and saw the lights.

They were amazing, blue and red and gold icicles of light shimmering in the water. But across Tukey's Bridge was something more amazing still. The bean factory, on a jut of land at the cove's mouth, was like an ocean liner riding a swell and its reflection seemed formed by silver crystals of light. The B and M bean factory: a crystal palace.

I walked and the smells in the air changed: a whiff of the bread factory across the cove at the foot of the Hill, a whiff of some sweet-smelling plant, then a rush of cold, bracing air sweeping right in through the cove's mouth direct from the Atlantic. The stars and a lumpy moon hung way up in the sky and down below, here on the path, runners ran and walkers walked, people passing each other in the night said hello, petted each other's dogs, sat on the benches and watched the lights on the water.

Tranquility or the appearance of tranquillity. Safety or the illusion of safety. Happiness or merely the absence of unhappiness. I wanted something very badly, but I didn't know what I wanted. Or I did, but I was afraid to think its name.

ૐ ૐ ૐ

Wilson wasn't in the office Monday morning when I came in to pick up a file and check the answering machine. There were a couple of calls on it: one from Luke ("Sorry. It's Sunday morning and only lawyers and other ministers of God work on Sunday mornings. I'll try you at home.") and one from Peter Lawrence ("It's Monday morning, 7:30. We're going to be in Ogunquit for a few days. The number there is...").

That blasted *we* again.

A ray of sunlight coming through the blinds was shining directly on the amethyst crystal on my desk. The light rippled over the stone, making it shimmer the way the reflections of light had shimmered on the water of the cove. It was like something living, but unearthly. An odd idea, since it was more of the earth than anything else, had been mined from the very insides of the earth. But that such color could exist underground, hidden from all sight, buried in a rock that someone had to go down and dig up, break open and reveal through brute force...that was just what we did, Wilson and I. We dug in the dirt, too, we ripped things open, we revealed what was hidden. If only the truth we found was always crystalline: that beautiful, that rewarding.

ૐ ૐ ૐ

I left Wilson a long detailed note with Luke's instructions and little maps. (Turn at the boulder. Look for a house with blue shutters and one of those white kittens stuck on the eaves...) I was driving up to the Bath Iron Works to talk to some welders about a jumper, some guy who had taken a leap off a crane. Never let anyone tell you being a private eye isn't glamorous work.

Bath is forty minutes from Portland, and on a nice day it's a pretty ride. You pass the B and M bean factory for one thing, and get a noseful of baked beans; then you're treated to a view of Casco Bay and the islands, then the marshes and the Royal River, then fields and woods. It reminds me that Portland is still a city in the country. Though you can certainly see urban sprawl to the south, housing developments and industrial parks where a few years ago there were woods and farm land, to the north and west it's still pretty rural. The coast is an endangered species, of course, but for the time being as you drive north and east from Portland, you can still imagine that Maine is remote enough from the rest of the nation to avoid the fate of other formerly beautiful places, Long Island, for example. For another few years anyway.

Ten miles out of Portland a storm moved in, thick, dark clouds, thunder, hail the size of golf balls. It was impossible to see two feet ahead even with headlights on and so when the intrepid pick-up in front of me (with the bumper sticker, I Brake for Hake) pulled over, I pulled over right behind him. We have been reduced to this: two seasons, the snowy season and the rainy season.

By the time the storm rock 'n rolled its way south and we could all drive at seventy again, it was lunch time. I tooled into the shipyard an hour late, but it was fine. I got the grand tour of our newest warships in their various stages of construction and got the dope on the jumper who, it seemed, had more reasons to check out than you could shake a stick at. A nice guy though. A real nice guy.

Instead of driving back to town I picked up a beer and an Italian (sandwich) and drove down the long finger of land from Bath to Popham Beach. The road winds and curls, rises and falls, passes fishing villages and farms. The fragrances in the air after the storm were intoxicating—sweet grass and pine trees and the sea. All the colors seemed newly washed—deep greens, deep blues, a patch of yellow buttercups in a field, a bright red lobster trap, a deeper red barn. At the end of the road, the very end, were white sand dunes and wild roses and sweet peas and an azure blue sea.

I sat in the sand and ate my lunch. Not many people on the beach today, and those who were were walkers, not sun bathers. The ocean was sparkling in the sun, vast, stretching out forever. I find the ocean calming, as long as I'm not in it, and I let it calm me enough so I could think about murder again.

It was hard to do. My mind kept focusing on the human detail, not on the holy trinity of homicide investigations: means, motive and opportunity. Yes, Peter had the means and the opportunity and maybe the motive. Possibly so did Jonathan. But it wasn't my job to make a case against either one of them; the cops were supposed to be doing that.

And if homicide detectives operated the way BIDE agents did, the way Luke Neville described someone like Vince Scully, for example, if they were that good at lying, entrapping, dealing and intimidating, then eventually somebody would give them Peter Lawrence, somebody would have to.

Will was right; I was far too emotionally involved. I had to put everything I felt aside, everything I knew or thought I knew, and go looking for Michelle, even up in the blueberry barrens of Washington County if need be. Or else just leave it. I had talked to almost everybody on the list...not that the list was going to help. I had done what Gareth was paying me to do, so why shouldn't I stop while we were all ahead? Peter might have better luck with a jury than any of us imagined. Given a little inducement, he could probably seduce the heart out of a piece of farm equipment.

Before I left the beach, I rolled up my pants and ran bare legged into the surf. Ice water. Like love, the Atlantic often looks better than it feels.

Chapter 18

By the time I got back to the office, it was after four. Still no Wilson. No Wilson, no note, no nothing. I rewound the tape and settled down to listen to the plaintive voices of my clients asking me where the hell I was: Johnson. Moore. Bouchard. Then...

"Jo, if you're there pick up!... Hell, you're not there." Wilson. "OK, here's the scoop. It's 3:30. I'm in Bridgton. At the pizza joint on Main Street. Love to see your pretty profile here, hon. We got business in Waterford tonight. I'm leaving here now, but I'll check back in at six. *Try* to make it. If not, I'll be going from here to Perkins Orchards in Waterford. It's off 35 between Waterford and Lynchville. No kidding. You'll see the orchard sign. Don't turn there. Go another quarter mile or so and you'll see a turn-off for some camps. I'll wait for you there. Bring the baby and make sure she's loaded. If you don't get this message by 7, it'll be too late and I'll see you in the A.M. Bye."

It was 4:30. Rush hour on 302. If I busted my ass I might just make it to Bridgton by 6.

A strange time of year to go apple picking, Will, I thought. Then I dug out the baby and loaded her up with film.

❧ ❧ ❧

"They're going to be off-loading tonight," Wilson whispered to me like a conspirator while cramming pepperoni pizza into her mouth. "We need to go and take pictures."

"Why do we need pictures?"

"Blackmail."

"Great. Now we're blackmailers. What's next? Forgery? Larceny?"

"Freer's girlfriend..." Wilson swallowed her mouthful and took a long pull on her soda,"...besides being adorable is scared shitless. Everybody in town is scared shitless. The whole county may be..."

"Scared. OK, I think I got it."

"She knows who killed Freer. Freer's brother, who is holed up in the woods somewhere, knows who killed Freer..."

"The whole damn county knows who killed Freer. And I take it nobody's telling."

"Too scared."

I sighed. Wilson gets like this sometimes. The cat who swallowed the canary along with the pepperoni.

"Courtney," she said, gulping, "Freer's girlfriend, knew about this shipment. Told me after much persuasion and a lot of instant coffee and Newport menthols. I didn't think anybody smoked Newport..."

"Pot?"

"A ton. Two thousand pounds. Freer set up the deal a few months ago. Then something happened. One of those wrinkles. Another outfit wanted in. He said no way..."

"And those guys stiffed him?"

"Sounds likely."

"But the deal's still going down?"

"Tonight. What's the street price per pound these days?"

"No idea. I'm strictly a retail buyer. I'm not even up to whole ounces. Half ounce maybe, if I'm feeling flush."

"Well, say the street price an ounce is one fifty, that's twenty-four hundred a pound, right? Selling wholesale, say two thousand a pound, multiplied by two thousand pounds... Four million?"

"Jesus Christ."

"It's not harvest time around here, so this must be imported shit."

"They must be trucking it here from the coast... So let me see if I get this. We're going to take pictures of some guys unloading two thousand pounds of pot. And why are we doing this? You don't expect Freer's killer to show up, do you?"

"No. But I think Freer's people might be more willing to talk to us if we have pictures of them committing a major felony."

"But, Will, the bales will be wrapped up in burlap or something. There'll be no way of proving what they're unloading."

"We'll get something incriminating, don't worry."

"This is low profile, huh? What does Courtney say about Luke's client, what's his name?"

"Matt Perkins."

"The orchard Perkins?"

"Related. Everybody up here's related... She says he never killed Bobby. Wanted to beat the shit out of him, maybe, but..."

"Was he in on this deal, too?"

"Until their falling out. Money and a woman."

"Ah, the big two. Courtney?"

"No. Matt was dating Freer's ex-wife and accused Freer of still sleeping with her. Which Courtney says is a load of bull."

"So who inherited Freer's import/export company?"

"His ex-brother-in-law. Guy named Bill Morris."

"And he'll be there tonight?"

"With bells on, I imagine. Stashing a bit of weed in the barn. I hope it's a big barn. And I hope you got high speed film."

I sat and watched Wilson devour her fourth slice of pizza. I didn't have much of an appetite, but I kept nibbling on my own first slice to keep her company. She was in her element on this case. Wilson was born to be a general of an invading army. She didn't know what fear was, physical fear anyway. There she sat, the picture of cool in white rayon, putting away pizza and thinking about film speed. Not bullet velocity. Not how many nine millimeters might be on those guys stashing pot in their barn. No. Drug smugglers, millions in marijuana, an isolated orchard and the two of us with our high speed film. Just another picnic in the country.

ða ða ða

We parked Wilson's car on the side of the dirt road just past the turn-off for Perkins Orchards, and Wilson dug around in her trunk for a black trench coat.

"Camouflage," she said.

"Well," I said. "Clearly we should have brought my car. *My* car's trunk is full of jungle combat fatigues."

"Scare me," she said.

We walked a little way back along 35 to the turn-off to the orchard and saw we had quite a hike ahead of us. There were acres of apple trees between us and the farmhouse and barn.

"Secluded," I said.

"Perfect stash house. Until apple season anyway."

It was actually a very fine night for a walk in the country. The moon was gibbous, ripening, the air was fresh if a little on the frigid side, and Wilson was next to me. In fact, it would have been a perfect night for a walk in the country if I wasn't expecting a truck to turn in and barrel down on us at any moment. We hugged the shoulder under the shadow of the trees, getting our feet wet, keeping our eyes open, expecting the worst. They, we hoped, weren't expecting anything except a truckload of grass and so had no reason to be tip-toeing around their own property. Unless they had guard dogs, we'd hear them long before they'd hear us.

᙭ ᙭ ᙭

As we got closer we could make out the farmhouse and behind it and to the left, the barn. Farther left, on a slight hill overlooking the orchard, was another building or cluster of buildings, weirdly shaped, baroque, like a series of towers and domes. There were a few pick-ups in the yard, a horse in the back field, the smell of animals and wet earth and a wood stove. Lights were on in the main house; the barn was closed up and dark.

We stopped in the shadows, the grotesquely twisted shapes of apple trees all around us. I wanted a cigarette but knew a cigarette was the last thing I could have. Not till we were safely back on the road. Jungle combat rules.

"They'll pull the truck right into the barn," Wilson whispered. "We have to get inside before they do."

I stared up the dirt road: house, barn, pick-ups, shapes without color, as though the things themselves were somewhere else and had left only shadows of themselves behind. And the breeze was kicking up, the trees rustling, everything ghostly and undefined, only half-present. I couldn't see the red of Will's hair or the green of her eyes.

"How?" I whispered back.

"We'll figure it out. Come on."

I followed her through the trees until we were as close as we could get to the barn and still remain hidden. We'd have to creep along now, finding shadows, dark places. Make our way to the side of the barn and then feel around for a door. But there were other outbuildings they could use or we could. I really didn't like the idea of being trapped in that barn.

I was about to make the argument for staying out of the barn when the question became moot. Headlights were coming toward us along the road. We made a dash for the nearest shelter, a shed. The door wasn't locked. Wilson whispered something about staying out to watch the truck, but I wouldn't listen and pushed her through the door.

It was black inside, smelt of fertilizer and motor oil. If we moved an inch, I was convinced we'd knock over a shovel or slit our throats on a scythe. The truck was right in the yard now; a splinter of light slipped through the crack in the door and passed on. We could hear men's voices, the car doors slamming shut, the engine idling. We could hear just fine, but we weren't going to see much from where we were.

"I'll go out," I said. "Keep me covered."

Wilson pinched my arm. The pinch meant: keep me covered, indeed! You've been watching too many episodes of Miami Vice, honey.

I opened the door a crack and looked out. Everything was brighter; they had turned on some lights to illuminate the barnyard. And there was activity over there as well. Only problem was there was also a panel truck parked smack dab in my way. I took the baby out of my pocket and hugging the shed moved along the wall toward the yard. The baby is really an almost top-of-the-line surveillance camera, one of those James Bond fantasy jobs that modern technology has placed within reach of ordinary mortals: a camera as small as a pack of cigarettes with the capabilities of a spy satellite. Automatic everything. All I had to do was aim, but I had to have something to aim at.

I made it to the end of the wall and very cautiously checked out the panel truck. The cab was empty. I crept along the side of it until I got to the rear end where I could finally get a clear view of the scene in the yard.

A pick-up was positioned to back into the barn as soon as the barn doors were opened. Two men were working on the doors, and the driver was hanging out the window waiting for the go-ahead. I could see them all pretty well in the light; the baby would see them a lot better. I put the camera to my eye and snapped: driver, first doorman, second...

A footfall behind me. I palmed the camera just as a heavy hand came down on my shoulder.

"Motherfucker. Who the fuck are you?"

Oh, shit.

Chapter 19

I turned around—actually it was more like being spun around—and faced a very big, very bearded and very angry man. Beside and a little behind him, like an emaciated shadow, stood a second man with a beard as long as my arm. The angry man pushed me up against the van and hissed at me, something about trespassers and spies, and I knew I had to either start a lightning rap about my car running out of gas on the road or wait for Wilson to come out shooting. But the skinny shadow man had taken a step forward and was holding his hand out to me.

"Hey, lighten up," he said chuckling (yes, chuckling!) to the giant. "This is my old friend Mary Lou. Hey, how ya doin'?"

"Fine," I said. And shook the giant's hand off my shoulder. "Sort of fine."

"Shit, Kenny," the giant muttered. "What the fuck. You didn't tell me you had a guest."

"It's OK, man. She's a cool lady. Mary Lou, this is Bill."

"Hi, Bill," I said. Yes, I thought, and welcome to the Twilight Zone.

"Come on with me. I'll make you some tea. Hope you haven't been waiting long. Have you?" And Kenny took my arm and led me away from the panel truck and the barnyard lit like a stage, back in the direction of the road. I caught a final glimpse of the shed, the barn, the pick-up, the man tossing bales of marijuana off the bed into waiting arms...one final look over my shoulder in Wilson's direction, before Kenny steered me to a path that led toward the cluster of weirdly shaped buildings, one of which was most definitely a geodesic dome.

ɞ ɞ ɞ

He didn't say another word, nor did I, until we were inside. But inside what? We crossed something like a wooden bridge and entered what was clearly a mud room, a room set aside for foul weather gear, boots or skis or snowshoes. From the mud room we went through a door into a room that was many-sided, hexagonal maybe, or octagonal, with a peaked roof, constructed out of rough-hewn wood. There were many things in this room: lots of books and papers, an old A.B. Dick printing press, a wood stove, a rocking chair. I followed him through another doorway and into the spaciousness of the dome. This space was kitchen and living area: an overstuffed couch, a braided rug, a cooking stove and a sink, a kitchen table, herbs hanging upside down to dry. Other passages off this room led further into this strange house. To a sauna maybe or the tower.

Kenny gestured for me to take a seat at the table, and he filled a kettle with water using a hand pump at the sink. "Gas stove," he said, like he was apologizing for something. He lit the gas with a match and set the kettle on top. "Got some chamomile, sassafras, red zinger, Constant Comment, mint. What's your pleasure?" He spoke so slowly you could fall asleep between words.

I said mint would be nice. He agreed. Would I like honey? Local hive. Good. I said honey would be lovely. Then I said, "Kenny, my name isn't Mary Lou."

"Ayuh," he said. "We'll be gettin' to that. In due time. Get the tea brewin' first." He went up to a cabinet filled with different shaped jars of herbs and teas, incense, who knows what, and started sorting through, looking, I assumed, for the mint. A fat coon cat jumped onto my lap and made himself comfortable. Kenny asked if I'd like to hear some music.

I was beginning to think he was one of those lunatic hermits every Maine family seems to keep buried in a shed in the woods. Enough mystery. I introduced myself. I even said I was a private detective. Just to set the record straight.

He had meanwhile found the right jar, set it on the table, pulled a chair out and sat down across from me. He took a package of Drum out of his shirt pocket and Zigzags and began to roll himself a cigarette. I wondered if he had even heard me. I was about to offer him a ready-rolled just to see if he would react when he said, "Yup. Courtney asked me to look out for you. Thought she said the name was Ruth..."

There was a terrific noise behind me. I jumped in my chair, but the cat on my lap didn't move, so I couldn't even get up to face whatever it was that had just kicked the door in. All I could do was turn in my chair and hope...

Wilson was standing in her shooting stance, pistol pointed right at Kenny's mandarin beard. "Don't move a goddamn muscle," she said.

"And this is my partner," I said. "Ruth Wilson. Will, this is

Kenny."

"Pleased to meet you, Ruth. Just makin' some tea. Care for a cup?"

ðə ðə ðə

The tea was getting cold in our cups, but we had moved on to Jim
Beam as soon as Wilson sat down and made a few well chosen and
highly disparaging remarks about mint tea with honey. Kenny was an
obliging host.

His name was Kenny Perkins and it was his family's orchard we
had strolled through that evening. Bob Freer had been his best friend.
Kenny had always let Bob use the barn for his stash, so long as it wasn't
filled with apples. Kenny's cut was the shake. His dad didn't approve
exactly, didn't much mind either. It was just another plant to him.

Kenny talked so slowly, with so many elongated pauses between
question and answer, that I thought poor Wilson was going to start
jumping out of her skin. She kept asking direct questions like, "Who
killed Bobby Freer?" Kenny kept giving her answers that began with
the Flood, worked through the Indian Wars, curled around Prohibition
and meandered lazily through the '60's, Vietnam, the coming of the
people from away...

He was getting to it.

The good old days. Before cocaine.

Sandoz and blotter acid. Psilocybin. Mescaline. Hash. Michoacan.
Communes. Yurts. His pick-up with the dome on the back.

"About Bobby..."

He was getting to it.

He and Bobby had moved to Portland, but they couldn't handle
living in a city. Came back here and built their houses and settled in.
Kenny started a small press, published poetry. Worked in the orchard,
helped his dad. Bobby got married, had a kid, got divorced. Worked as
a carpenter, could make anything with his hands. Grew pot for awhile
but got busted. Airplanes. Helicopters. They used airplanes and helicopters like it was fucking Vietnam. So he couldn't grow pot, but he
could buy it in bulk, sell it to his friends. Never smuggled weed in
himself, but bought it from local growers or importers. Never dealt
with outsiders.

But outsiders started dealing with him. The urban markets were
tied up, but that didn't matter; they were strictly rural distributors
anyway. But the city networks spread. All of a sudden their own buyers
were saying Bobby was ripping them off, they could get better prices

from other folks. Better weed, too.

Then—this is two months ago maybe—there's no weed in the state. None. Demand is astronomical; prices are out of sight. Two hundred, three hundred an ounce. Four hundred an ounce. And it's five months until harvest. Bobby hears about this shipment, a couple of tons. Can he handle two thousand pounds? Sure can. He makes the arrangements. Then he starts hearing from these thugs. Through the grapevine at first, then phone calls. Then one of them shows up at his place. He's not to touch this grass. He's to retire. Retire! Like who the fuck is this asshole, telling Bobby Freer to fucking retire?

Next thing, Bobby's chopped up in a field.

"Did Bobby know these guys who came to talk to him?"

"Not too likely he'd know 'em, seein' as how they were from away." Kenny paused and I could almost feel Wilson clenching her teeth. "But he did tell me their names."

Wilson took a very deep breath, like she'd been holding it for the last five minutes.

"This is how I see it," Kenny said in his slow drawl. He was stuffing tobacco into his pipe while he talked, and he really couldn't do both things at once. Wilson was turning red, but maybe it was from the whiskey. "You two are working for Matt's lawyer. I tell you who these guys are and you tell him. Then he deals with it, right? I didn't meet these men. I didn't talk to these men. Bobby told me about them and Bobby's dead. He might 'a told twenty other people as well as me. I don't know. But Bob Freer was my friend, and I'll tell you this, if I knew where those motherfuckers were now I'd go shoot 'em myself. But they're probably back in Medellin." He pronounced it Medal-lynn.

"Colombians," Wilson said, like it was something she already knew.

"One did all the talking. Other one just stood around. Silent one was the creepy one. Never got his name. But the talker, Bobby got his name all right. Zola. Like the French writer. Zola."

He sat rocking in the rocking chair, beard in his lap, pulling on his tobacco pipe. Zola. Al Zola. Fuck a duck.

"The Feds," Wilson said slowly, carefully, "just busted a coke dealer in Lovell by the name of Alzola. Story's been all over the Portland papers. Photos too."

"Lovell, eh? But these guys were from away, I told ya. Mass. plates."

Wilson smiled across the table at him. "I think Matt's lawyer can do something with this," she said. "And for somebody willing to shoot the bastards that killed Bobby, talking to the Feds'll be duck soup."

"All I got is gossip," he said. "But Bill now...he seen the bastards with his own eyes..."

❧ ❧ ❧

Before we left, Kenny presented us both with books of poetry he had published on his press and a few jars of apple butter. He even walked us back up the road to the car. In as much as it was possible to judge from such slight evidence, he seemed pleased. We had promised to talk to Luke; we had promised not to implicate him by name. But I had the feeling that Kenny Perkins was going to turn hero on us pretty soon. It was percolating in there. Just give it some time.

And we had the photographs for back-up. Alzola was going to the wall if we had to drag him there by his balls.

❧ ❧ ❧

Will had to concentrate driving those thirteen miles along the back roads to Bridgton, where I had left my car. She had the highbeams on, but it was still easy to lose your way, miss a signpost or surprise a deer in the road, or even a moose. So we drove without saying too much. Just the obvious stuff:

Strange guy.

Nice though.

Al Zola. Well, shut my mouth!

Luke will be happy as a clam at high tide.

While we were passing these remarks back and forth in the dark, Wilson reached across the seat and took my hand and held it until she had to downshift five miles or so outside of town.

Chapter 20

Wilson beat me back to Portland. I found her in my kitchen making coffee. It was almost midnight.

"We have to talk," she said.

"It's late. Let's talk tomorrow."

"That's why I'm making coffee."

"Great," I said and took off my shoes.

"If Alzola's our man, you know what that means?"

"Yeah. It means if he was in Bridgton killing Bob Freer on Saturday night, he couldn't be in Portland killing José Ruiz. Remind me to remind the cops to check out that Beretta in the glove compartment of the Alpha Romeo. Just on the off chance that he's dumb enough to hold onto a gun he killed somebody with."

"Right. But listen, Jo. It took more than one man to pull off that murder. Alzola *and* Ruiz were in Bridgton Saturday night."

"OK. Then what happened?"

"They come back to town together. Ruiz picks up Michelle, or maybe she's his old lady from Boston and she's up here to vacation with him on Kezar Lake. Anyway they meet up, and Ruiz starts bragging about this murder in Bridgton, shooting off his mouth. Alzola figures the guy's a liability, he's gotta go. Now Luke says they tortured Freer, right? Maybe they wanted information from him. Maybe they got Peter Lawrence's name from him. They want to crack the Portland market, that's evident right? They want exclusive rights to the Portland market, and they want to oust the little guys, the Freers and the Boulangers and the Lawrences. Right? So they get Peter's name and address from Freer—this is all speculative but possible—with the idea that they're going to do a little knee-capping down the road. But then Alzola gets this great idea..."

"Oh, Jesus."

"Listen, it doesn't have to be true. It just has to be possible. The AG isn't as smart as you are. The AG just wants a sexy conviction, and

Alzola may just be an easier lay."

"But Alzola didn't kill Ruiz. I know he didn't."

Wilson yawned and poured each of us a cup of very thick, very black coffee which I had no intention on earth of drinking. "I think you are identifying a mite too much, Jo. If you don't mind my saying so. What is this, a familiar plot from a classic Russian tragedy or something? Does this remind you of a famous ballet? Revenge killings and crimes of passion? This can't be simple gangster shit, right? This has to be..."

"Wilson. I saw Peter in the Oaks last night. He was with a woman. A small blonde woman. But it wasn't a woman. It was Jonathan. I'm sure it was Jonathan."

"May I be forgiven, dear God, for ever suggesting this idea to her..."

"Tomorrow I'm going over to Peaks to talk to Peter's ex-whatever. She must know Jonathan pretty well. Zoe was with them last night and she must mention it. Like, Jonathan's gender bending again, Mom... Also I'd like a realistic picture of Peter Lawrence for once. From somebody who doesn't think he's a fucking saint."

"Fine. You go talk to Michelle of the Dark Hair. Then what?"

"Then I know. I just want to know." (Dig it out of the ground, pry it open, see the color of the crystal inside...)

"Maria Santos' case is going to hell in a handbasket, too, if it's any consolation to you. Solange is not going to testify."

"And you couldn't persuade her? Not after a whole night? I *am* surprised."

"We have to talk," Wilson said again.

"We are talking."

"I'm in love."

I was sitting at the table; she was leaning against the counter by the coffee pot. We were less than three feet away from each other, but even so I felt as though a crack in the earth had just opened up between us. Wilson announced she was in love like other women announced they were pregnant: rarely and only after the fact was positively and scientifically confirmed.

"That's great," I said. "I wish I had some champagne in the house." But I was thinking, will you please go home now? Will you please, please go home?

Wilson covered the distance between us in one little step, took my face in her hands, bent over and kissed me. It was a real kiss and a pretty crumby time for it, too, I thought. A real sweet, long good-bye kiss.

I pulled away from her. "What was that for?"

"I just figure I've been waiting long enough."

"*You've* been waiting? I think you should go home to poor Solange. It's almost one o'clock in the morning, and she looks like she might be the fiercely possessive type. And if you're in love with her, what are you doing kissing me?"

"Solange is a fruitcake," Wilson said. She pulled up another chair and sat down across from me, knee to knee. "She's not living on the same planet we are. On her planet they speak a different language, and it's like they're tripping all the time and having Great Insights which they like to share with you if you're in the vicinity. So her Great Insight about me was that I'm not very happy but put up a good front, and the reason I'm not very happy is because my life is on hold while I wait for someone to decide to love me again, someone who's an ice maiden on the outside but a marshmallow underneath. And that I'll be waiting forever if I don't go for broke now."

"Did she do all this with crystals?"

"Crystals and runes and wands. She's a walking light and magic show, a regular gypsy caravan. But this particular information came from Tarot cards."

"Since when do you listen to Tarot cards?"

"Since they started telling the truth."

"What truth? That you're in love with a frozen marshmallow?"

"I took it to mean you."

"Oh," I said. Stunned. I had been so mesmerized by my mental image of Wilson and Solange LaBelle (I had dreamt it: the two of them waltzing together, one in white silk, one in black leather) that this declaration came at me completely from left field, like that car running a red light that you bang into because it's just not supposed to be there. And the old fear started tightening itself into a nice hard knot in my throat. It lives somewhere in that region, sleeps in the esophagus like a dragon in its cave.

"And then tonight, driving back to Bridgton with you...it suddenly hit me... Why Alzola brought you out to the lake that night. What he wanted." Wilson's voice was getting husky; it was so late, and she'd been talking for hours... "He and Ruiz had killed Freer, and then you show up with a photo of Ruiz. Maybe you're a P.I., yeah, but who are you working for? The growers? Big Bill Morris? And if so, how much do you know? How much do they know? Alzola wanted information from you, and how was he planning to get it? Look at what he did to Freer. A coroner's report Luke Neville couldn't even read through..."

"Well," I said. I tried to smile at her. I was beginning to feel like I could breathe again, but I wasn't sure I could smile. "Nothing like being terrified in retrospect."

She reached over and took my hands. "I just think it's time for us to give it another try. Maybe let our shields down a little, Jo. Take some of the armor off. See if we're still the same sex maniacs underneath." She tried to smile, but it looked like it was as hard for her as it had been for me. "Because I really love you," she said.

"You really loved me last time, too," I said.

"We're smarter now, don't you think? We could pull it off this time."

"What if we can't? What if it turns out that we just can't be lovers and partners at the same time?"

"Nick and Nora Charles managed."

"They were rich and had a dog."

"So we'll win the lottery. And we'll get a dog...Whatever you want. I love you. So if you think we need a dog..."

I didn't know if I was about to laugh or cry, and I was saved from deciding because the phone started to ring.

The Midnight Caller...or somebody else. I picked up the receiver. "I'm holding my dick in my hand," he whispered into my ear. "I'm stroking it..." I sighed, as I usually do—acknowledgment if not encouragement—and gently replaced the receiver. He's polite, never calls more than once a week, never too much after midnight.

"Nobody," I said. "Kids. Where were we?"

"A dog. Astor. Nick and Nora Charles. Marriage after a long engagement."

This time I did smile at her, and this time she did smile back. "Right," I said. "I'll think about it."

"Before we go to Lisbon?"

"All right. Before we go to Lisbon. Did Solange see a trip in your future too?"

"Oh, that reminds me. I have something for you." She got up and returned to the table with a slim book in her hand. "From Solange. *Crystals Even a Christian Could Love.* Or some such thing. Check under A for Amethyst. You know, Solange may be way out there in bliss ninnyhood, but she could almost convince you..."

"Wilson," I said, "remember who you're talking to."

"Skeptic of the Century. Yes, I remember..."

The phone rang again. My Midnight Caller never abuses his phone privileges like this. I pulled my whistle out of the cabinet drawer and picked up the phone. But luckily I didn't blow his eardrums out. Luckily because it was Kenny Perkins.

"Found that newspaper with the photograph you were talkin' about," he said in his low, flat drawl. "Showed it to Billy, and he says that's never Zola. Got his name underneath it all right, but t'ain't him. It's the other one."

I transmitted this to Wilson and asked Kenny if Billy had anything else to say.

"Just what he'd like to do to the pig fucker. He's wicked mad."

"Mad enough to come into Portland and I.D. the real Alzola? They got him or somebody who claims to be him in the county jail right now, though he could make bail tomorrow."

Pretty likely Billy'd come into town for that, Kenny figured, Billy currently being mad as a wet hen. I gave him Luke Neville's number while Wilson dumped our coffee into the sink and refilled our cups with the last of my vodka. I finished talking to Kenny in my calmest voice, lay down the receiver and yelled, "Got him!"

"Yahoo!" Wilson yelled back, and we did a little victory jig around the table. "Solange was right! All we needed were the right rocks."

"Wilson!" I said, grabbing her by the shoulders and shaking her. "Stop!"

"I'm going out tomorrow to buy us crystals. Lots and lots of pretty crystals."

"And I will brain you with one of them."

"Choose your weapon!" she said, dangling the crystal book in front of me.

"OK. I give. Read to me about amethyst."

I sat down and listened to her read: "Amethyst. A powerful blood cleanser and energizer. Strengthens the endocrine and immune systems. Is associated with healing involving the head. Cures migraines. Helps mental disorders. Enhances right brain activity. Purifier and regenerator on all levels of consciousness. Transmutes the lower nature into the more highly refined aspects of higher potential. Cuts through illusion. Enhances psychic ability. Has calming and protective qualities... Oh, God, Jo, this is the best. *For clear understanding of death and rebirth, lie on your back and place the crystal on your forehead.*"

"Peter's sure got a great sense of humor," I said.

"You know what else Solange told me?"

"I see a dark man, an artist, gentle, faithful, falsely accused. The Knight of Wands beside Justice reversed." Wilson looked impressed. "My mother read cards and tea leaves," I said. "It's in my genes."

"Hmm. Yes...well wasn't there another neighbor you wanted to check out?"

"The night owls across the street."

"OK. So you spin out your useful fiction and I'll spin out mine. You go to Peaks and ask Ms. Michelle..."

"It's odd that Jonathan would use her name, isn't it?"

"Odd is not the word for this fantasy of yours. But go ahead. Chase the wild goose over on Peaks. Ask about Jonathan's taste in lingerie. Make a fool out of yourself. I, on the other hand, will interview the night owls. If we can get one witness who'll testify to seeing two people go into that house before 4:30 Sunday morning while we've got Peter safely tucked into bed with Jonathan Hall..."

"Assuming Jonathan Hall was safely tucked into bed with Peter..."

"It doesn't matter. If we can get a witness and Jonathan sticks to his story, Peter is off the hook. That's what we're getting paid for, right? That's what you want, isn't it? Isn't it what you want?"

The last sentence sounded so sexy I was about to tell her that I had thought about her proposal long enough and she shouldn't bother going home, not now, not ever, but I was also so tired I thought I was going to fall into a coma at any moment. I must have looked it to. "Go to bed now," she said. She leaned over and kissed me again and then she smiled, as though patience now was the better part of valor. "Tomorrow is another day."

I watched her pick up her briefcase and black (camouflage) trench coat and saunter to the door. My dick. My very own private dick.

"Have a wicked good time on Peaks," she said. And she gave me one of those over-the-shoulder Wilson grins, Cheshire-cat-like, and sauntered out into the night.

Chapter 21

I'd never admit it, but I love taking the ferry to Peaks. Longtime residents are supposed to be inured to such things: the excitement on the dock, the boarding, the deck hands casting off the lines, the captain's warning before the long whistle, the first thrilling blast of real sea air, the sound of the buoys that mark the straits. No, to a coastal Mainer boats are just like cars, the water is just another road, and what fool's ass oohhs and aahhs over an old Ford pickup tooling down Route 1? The boat to Peaks isn't even in the pickup league. To a native the ferry is only a floating version of a city bus.

But this city bus is yellow and white with red trim, red benches on deck and a red and white canopy over the stern and is named Island Romance. You can sit on deck and watch the red brick city recede, noticing how neatly it rises up, hugging its spine of land, a neck to the British, who called it Falmouth Neck, a knee to the Indians, who called it Machigonne, or Bent Knee. Turning away from the city so that the sea breeze hits your face, a stiff breeze usually, once the ferry moves out of the harbor, you can see a scattering of green islands appear, the summits of drowned mountains, and beyond them the Atlantic stretching out to England. Island Romance chugs along past the big blue dry dock of the Bath Iron Works, Portland division; past the pleasure boats and the tankers in the harbor; past grass-covered Fort Gorges, built before the Civil War and across Hussey Sound as though it were heading right through Whitehead Passage and into the open sea...but it doesn't. It chugs along safe inside the Bay, passing lobster buoys and lobster boats pulling traps and yachts bobbing at anchor, chugging right along toward the rickety Peaks Island dock where the island's only taxi waits and kids jostle each other to be the first to jump off the pier into the departing ferry's wake. You might as well be crossing a time zone as well as a stretch of water, a major time zone, at that.

❧ ❧ ❧

Michelle Garner lived off Central Avenue midway between what islanders refer to as down front, the side of the island that faces the mainland, and back shore, which faces the sea. It was a simple white clapboard house with a pretty flower garden, a good sized vegetable plot and a noticeable absence of toys in the yard. When I spoke with her over the phone before I left home that morning, she had surprised me by seeming surprised herself that I would want to talk with her about Peter Lawrence. As though a call from a detective working for Peter's lawyer was the last thing she expected. As though hearing Peter's name was the last thing she expected. That should have clued me in, but I was mentally distracted—obsessing about Wilson, commitment, romance, adventure and how I would have to quit smoking now since Wilson would insist on long life without any preventable terminal illnesses. If Solange was doing my reading, she would have covered me with the High Priestess and crossed me with the Fool. The woman who interests the Querent and the future as yet unrevealed, obstructed by folly, mania, delirium and intoxication, or desire for same. In any case I hadn't paid too much attention to the tone of Michelle Garner's voice, so I was stunned by the woman who opened her front door to me. She was tall and reed thin, dark-haired, yes, though her hair was streaked with white. She had the disheveled, neglected appearance of someone who lives alone and doesn't expect to be surprised by visitors. And she was forty-five if she was a day.

I was shocked at myself for being shocked at Michelle Garner. I thought I was beyond gender tyranny, the attack of the internal gender fascists, Wilson calls it. So Peter had been involved with an older woman. So what? Young women get involved with older men all the time and nobody bats an eye. So why were my eyelids batting away like that?

"I'm so sorry I was rude to you on the phone this morning," she said. We were sitting on unbearably uncomfortable rattan chairs in her stark white living room. "I wasn't completely awake, and though I spoke to Peter just the other day, I wasn't really expecting you to call. I haven't seen much of him in some time."

Except on her walls of course. There were three of Jonathan's portraits of him hanging right in front of our noses.

"Did Peter call to warn you I was coming?" I smiled as sweetly as I could and watched her react to the word "warn."

"Well, yes, in a sense," she said, smiling sweetly back. "He said he had mentioned me as a character witness and that I might be hearing from his lawyer. If I didn't object, of course."

"And did you object?"

"Certainly not. I'm very fond of Peter."

Fond of him? This was beginning to feel like another one of those Twilight Zone conversations. And then it struck me that I might have this relationship all wrong, that it might have been one of those parenting arrangements that gay men and lesbians make, that Zoe's existence might be the whole goal and purpose of it, and that of course in that case they would be fond of each other. Why not? And if that were the case, I had just wasted my time and money trekking out here, though it was a nice day for a boat ride. So, playing as dumb as I felt, I asked her the "how long ago and under what circumstances you met" questions...the basics.

She'd known Peter ten years. He had been a student in one of her photo classes; they had become friends and remained friends. She knew Jonathan from his art school days, too, and actually knew him better since he had been a photo major, and she had been granted the status of confidante during his and Peter's long, ardent and involved court-ship, ordeal by courtship, Jonathan used to call it.

"And what is your opinion of Jonathan?"

"My opinion? I'm not sure you can have an opinion about some-one you care deeply about. I'm not sure an opinion is what I could give you. Maybe if you were more specific?"

"Is he a truthful person, do you think?"

"I'd say he's a truthful person, yes."

"His testimony is vital in this case, so it's important for us to know whether he's vulnerable to attack by the prosecution. Did he ever show any sort of aberrant behavior?"

"Aberrant behavior? Well, back in those days everybody who went to art school could be accused of aberrant behavior. And of course the school itself was a much wilder place ten years ago. Perhaps you remember..."

"No, I haven't lived here that long."

"Ah. Well, there were many social events at the school ten years ago which almost required aberrance as a condition of participation. The Halloween Party, for example, and the auction. It was *de rigeur* to appear at these functions in bizarre or obscene dress or in drag or as a walking work of art..."

"Jonathan was into cross dressing then?"

"I think it was in vogue at the time."

"And now?"

"Really I wouldn't know. Is cross dressing a sign of deception? Is a cross dresser to be considered untruthful? I'm just curious."

"No. But we don't want to be surprised about anything."

"I suppose you could simply ask him. Couldn't you?"

"Of course. And if he's a truthful person he'll tell me."

"*Touché*" she said, and asked me if I'd like something to drink.

ð ð ð

We drank iced tea, and I listened to Michelle talk about Jonathan's work, Peter's work, her own work, circling around the real subject, which I imagined she might have a more burning interest in than I did: whether or not the father of her child had committed murder. But Michelle seemed determined to remain detached from the entire issue, as though it were of no concern to her at all. I couldn't quite get a take on her. Her own takes on people, however, were thorough and eccentric. She thought Peter was rapidly bringing into union in his psyche the four great male archetypes of warrior, lover, magician and king. She was fascinated that he was doing it with such comparative ease, proving that the Jungian idea of the *animus/anima* and even the concepts of masculine and feminine transcended our limited notions of sexual identity, transcended physical gender entirely. She thought Jonathan overly eroticized his subjects and needed to begin working with other models besides Peter. She had many opinions, and they were all intriguing. I wondered what sort of mother this woman might be who struck me as one of those highly intellectual people who live so much in their minds they lose contact with their bodies and whom Wilson rather unkindly refers to as Brains With Feet. I wondered why Peter had made a child with her, and then I thought of his paintings, the long angular bodies, the geometric heads. Michelle, with her intellectual virtuosity and her sloppy housekeeping, was entirely unlike Jonathan, the object of Peter's sexual desire, but not so unlike the images he created in paint, the objects of his aesthetic desire. Maybe that was why.

We had talked for an hour, but still Zoe's name had not come up once. Had they agreed to keep her out of this? Was there some reason to? I had to find out. It was my job, after all, to find out.

"Tell me about Zoe," I said when the opening appeared. Nothing like the direct approach. "How is she dealing with all this?"

Michelle cocked her head a bit, as though she were listening to a voice speaking in the next room. "Zoe? Ah, Peter's daughter. I have no idea. I haven't seen Zoe...oh, in a year or more. You'd have to ask Peter about that. Or Zoe's mother. Michelle Nelson."

With that ingenuous statement, the house of cards I had been so meticulously constructing under the mistaken notion that I was building a case—against my own client, yes, but a case just the same—began to tremble. Not collapse entirely, but an architectural defect was clearly indicated.

"Michelle Nelson," I said. "Blonde, isn't she?"

"Well, that's a minimalist description if ever I heard one. She is blonde, yes. If you can imagine a female version of Jonathan, you'll have a pretty good notion of her physical appearance. Her resemblance to him has been made much of over the years, and for good reason, I think. Curlier hair though. As slender as he, but somewhat smaller. Also a photographer. She and Jonathan were in the same class; Peter was a few years ahead. What a pair they were, Michelle and Jonathan. Inseparable and such look alikes that when they wore each other's clothes you could barely tell them apart. And then poor Peter falling in love with both of them. Ah, youth! Thank God it doesn't last."

"So they look alike."

"They did, yes. And cultivated the look, too, I'd say. But that was years ago."

"I don't suppose they're friendly any more, Jonathan and Michelle?" I asked the question, but I was already gathering my things together. I had to find her, this Michelle Nelson, who may or may not have been with José Ruiz the night he died. A woman who certainly knew where Peter lived. A woman who might have any number of reasons to hate him. Though how she might have hooked up with someone like José Ruiz...

"Oh, there was a time when I expected them all to kill each other by turns, but that's ancient history now. The old saw that time heals all wounds, well, it's true enough. It was so intense for awhile that they split up. Peter went to San Francisco to study acting. Improv. Jonathan went to the East Village, and Michelle took Zoe and moved to Washington County, of all bizarre places, where she met and married an older man who—now imagine this!—turned out to be a cousin of Peter's. Cousin or second cousin, something like that. They were all reunited for the wedding and...well, the rest is history. But I do believe they are all firm friends now. And Zoe adores Jonathan, so..."

The house of cards was swaying now, on the verge of ruin. She moved to Washington County. She married an older man. He was Peter's cousin. The edge of enlightenment. Satori. When you see just what has been in front of you all the time. She married an older man. He was a pot grower.

"They have made an extended family for Zoe in the oddest sort of way. Almost by accident, I suppose. Or karma, depending on how you look at these things. Michelle's own family is a little weird from what I understand, but she married into this amazing clan, Peter's own clan, the whole leftover cast of the French and Indian Wars, as Jonathan puts it, all those Sackabasins and Sawyers and Neptunes and Atteans, Fourniers and Lawrences and Boulangers and St. Pierres. And Jonathan's family is quite wealthy, so Zoe will never be in any kind of financial need. Jonathan is such a Yankee, though. Sometimes I think he is genuinely horrified that he's gotten himself mixed up with..."

"She married Ray Boulanger," I said. It was a blunt statement of fact. My cards were scattered everywhere. Yet the odd thing was that though I had constructed a case based entirely on erroneous assumptions, I had the killer pegged right all along. Woman's intuition, I thought. Shit.

I told her I had to catch the boat, thanked her for her time and for the tea. I wanted to read the leaves, but there weren't any. Between instant tea and tea bags, it's no wonder our collective futures seem so bleak: there's nothing to read them by any more.

ᏋᏗ ᏋᏗ ᏋᏗ

Walking back to the dock past bathtub Madonnas and geraniums in tires and cats sunning themselves on front stoops, I thought about how I had made everything in this case more baroque than it was. That's our style, Wilson said. We like all those curlicues. But not Peter Lawrence. There was not a single gargoyle in any of his work.

I caught the noon boat back to the mainland. I sat on deck and watched the approaching city. And I let myself be amazed. Yes, he had amazed me after all. The conspiracy theory has always amazed and impressed me, even on paper. To think that somebody actually pulled it off, it was mind boggling. I let my mind be boggled all the way back to Portland. Then I went to the office to wait for Wilson. If I was right—and how could I not be?—she'd come through the door singing.

Chapter 22

Wilson was lying on her back on our fake Ming dynasty rug; Solange LaBelle was kneeling over her massaging her bare feet.

"Oh," Wilson said, though it was a pretty orgiastic "oh." "Here you are!"

Solange was wearing her usual bewitching black as well as half a dozen earrings in each ear and a load of pretty crystals on chains around her neck. Her head was newly shaved in the back and over her ears, and the hair on top was newly bleached to match the whiteness of her skin. She would have been scary if she wasn't so pretty. She was so pretty that her get-up seemed like poor costume design, like she was cast in a film with a lousy tech crew. No matter how you dressed her, Solange would always look—forgive the oxymoron—boyishly sweet.

Wilson propped herself up on her elbows and grinned at me. "Two short men went into Peter Lawrence's building at 1 A.M. last Sunday morning and half an hour later one of them came out. Alone. The Night Owls, Jo. We are golden."

"And how are they related to Peter Lawrence? Cousins? Grandparents? Ex-lovers?"

"Jesus, take a chill. They're just neighbors. What's the problem?"

I harumped at her and poured myself a cup of coffee. Wilson introduced me to Solange, who was still kneeling at her feet. What a picture.

"I thought you might be happy," Wilson said, a little petulantly. "We'll have some of that coffee too, if you don't mind."

"None for me," said Solange the Pure.

"Sorry," I said, Johannah the Nasty, "but we don't stock Celestial Seasonings. How about some bourbon?" Yes, I can be a surly bitch, but Wilson was grinning at me. She has a weakness for surly bitches.

"Solange is leaving town," Wilson said. "She came over to say goodbye. And give us a message for Maria."

And worship at your feet, I almost said. But didn't.

"Because I can't talk to her," Solange said. She had a heavy Queens accent which I found refreshing. At least she wouldn't say "wicked good," a phrase which represents the ultimate poetic expression in southern Maine colloquial speech. "I'm being blocked," Solange said.

"You mean the phone's always busy?"

"It's deeper than that," said Solange the Misunderstood.

By this time she and Wilson were sitting cross-legged on the rug. Rather than seem overtly reactionary and sit in a chair, I joined them. Solange placed her hands palms up on her black denim clad thighs and closed her eyes. Buddha in boots. Just don't let her start channeling, I prayed. Dear St. Jude, protect us from rubbernecking ghosts.

"She's not in a place where she can hear me right now," Solange said, incantation-style. "Maria feels powerless. She feels victimized. But she isn't a victim. She could empower herself. We are all aligned. She must let go. Just let go of them."

"Of her children, you mean?"

"We have worked side by side through many lifetimes. We are old souls. We have learned to love and trust each other, all three of us. We have been sister, husband, father, brother, lover to each other incarnation after incarnation. And Angela and Rafael, they also. The five of us..."

"Maria's kids," Wilson said to me *sotto voce*.

"Maria's and mine and Elise's," Solange corrected her. "In this life I've been both Maria's lover and Elise's. It's been very beautiful. But they have forgotten their essences. They can't remember who they are or why they are engaged in warfare over these children. But I can't fight against either one of them. I love them both, and so do Rafael and Angela. Luckily the children understand that when they chose Maria for their mother, they chose Elise as well."

"Hold it," I said. "You mean Rafael and Angela adopted Maria? What was she, at the mother pound?"

Solange gave me a truly beatific smile. "Yes, in a sense. We choose our parents, you know. We choose our race, gender, nationality. We need to work out certain things in this incarnation, and we know what environment will be best suited for the work we have to do. There is something we need to learn or accomplish..."

I understood what Wilson meant about Solange. She was a bliss ninny all right, living on another planet. And on this planet how convenient it must be to be a white upper class heterosexual male! He can congratulate himself on wise prenatal choices and live in the lap of luxury and power absolutely guilt-free. Oh, yes, during this incarnation I'm working on the problem of blue chip investments and learning all about the inner workings of Savings and Loans.

I pulled myself away from Solange's transcendent eye-contact to glance over at Wilson who, reading my mind as she often does, said, "So Maria needed to go to prison, and now she needs to lose custody of her kids, right?"

"She will be strengthened. She will learn non-possessiveness. These are her own choices. But it would be hard for me to say this to Maria."

"Right," said Wilson. "Especially in person. Maria might just break your jaw."

Solange straightened her legs and stretched down to touch her toes. "Maria believes that because she's Puerto Rican she will always be the victim of racism. She thinks Elise is a racist for taking her kids. Now if Elise was a racist why would she want two dark skinned Puerto Rican kids? Does that make sense? Maria's sure she's going to lose, too, because the courts are racist and homophobic and she's a lesbian and... Maria is so loaded down with negativity and rage and self-hatred... It's not good for kids, you know."

"So you think the kids are better off with Elise?"

"I think I did what I needed to do by bringing them to Elise. And Elise is doing what she needs to do by trying to keep them. And maybe in this process Elise and Maria will learn to cooperate with each other, maybe they'll have joint custody and will have to cooperate with each other. Love is operating here. Love brought the children to Elise... But Maria refuses love. She refuses love from anyone. She can't let herself be loved. It's very sad. People, you know, make their own tragedies. Just like they make their own diseases. You can't help them. They have to work on these problems themselves. They have to ask themselves why they are calling this or that particular strife onto themselves, or this particular illness. What it is they are looking for, why they need it."

"I hope you know how totally regressive this thinking is." I was trying not to sound furious, but I was furious. "This is like, why have a civil rights act? Why have medicine?"

"Well, yes," Wilson interrupted, "and I should warn you, Solange, that Wilder can break jaws, too, so maybe we'd better stop reading each other's auras and..."

"No, I want to know what Solange says to people with AIDS. That they called the virus into their bodies? That they want to die at nineteen or twenty-eight? That they need it? It's a fucking learning experience?"

Solange looked like she was receding into a deep trance, like she was about to start speaking in high pitched ancient Egyptian. It occurred to me that she'd make a lousy witness for Maria anyway. She looked too much like a punked out dyke and talked too much like a mental case. Maria was better off without her.

I had a phone call to make. I dialed Jonathan's number, raging. As a useful fiction for the oppressors of the world I guess it worked just dandy, this idea that we really wanted everything that happened to us, good or bad, and so nobody should feel responsible for anybody else's misery, because it wasn't really misery, it was a learning experience. But from the perspective of the oppressed, it had a familiar medieval ring to it. How smart of the elite to tell the peasants that they chose to be peasants. Any peasant who believed it probably deserved to stay a peasant, too.

The phone rang, but I didn't get Jonathan. What I got was a recording. "Hi. We're at Bob's house in Ogunquit for the week. The number there is..."

I dialed Bob's house in Ogunquit and got another recording. "Hi. You've reached the home of Bob Doucette and Charles Sewall. Neither of us can come to the phone right now, but if you will..."

I didn't bother to leave a message. I was an Amazon going into battle, and I didn't see any reason to give my opponent an advantage. Forewarned, after all, is forearmed.

Chapter 23

"You gonna tell me what's going down here, or is it billed as a Big Surprise?"

"Buckle up," I said. "We're going to Ogunquit."

Wilson fastened her seatbelt and slipped on her shades. By some miracle the sun was shining. "Yeah, well I got that much," she said. "I can read your aura pretty well, and it said OGUNQUIT, like a halo of letters all around..."

"We're going to confront Peter Lawrence."

"O.K. With what?"

"With a fiction. A nice useful fiction."

"All right. Which one?"

"That he killed José Ruiz. In the bedroom. With a rock."

"Oh," she said.

"See, there's one thing we forgot. Both of us. Peter Lawrence is an actor. And, God, what a great actor! Improv, Wilson. And what a troupe he's got working with him. Jonathan, the downstairs neighbors, the across-the-street neighbors, Michelle..."

"Whoa!" Wilson said, and just in time, too, since I was about to speed right by the entrance to the Maine Turnpike southbound. "So, Jonathan is a faithless drag queen after all? Everybody knows it, everybody knows Peter killed Ruiz in a fit of jealousy and now everybody's covering for him? This is the news from Peaks?"

"No," I said, accelerating up to a comfortable cruising speed. "The news from Peaks has nothing to do with Jonathan. The news from Peaks is that Michelle Garner is not Peter's ex. Peter's ex is another Michelle. A small blonde Michelle. Michelle Boulanger."

"Holy shit," said Wilson.

I smirked just a bit to myself, a very private smirk; I love to get a holy shit out of Wilson now and again.

"So Ray Boulanger's wife, who was so scared of the Mafioso, whose children were threatened...that woman is Michelle, small, blonde

Michelle, who was sending back drinks with José Ruiz in Gabriel's on the night of the murder..."

"And whose daughter is Zoe Neptune..."

"You can read this a bunch of different ways, Jo."

"I realize that. But I'm reading it as conspiracy. It's your useful fiction, Will, with a larger cast of characters."

"Visualize a motive," she said. "You know, I saw the greatest bumper sticker last week. You know those smug Visualize World Peace Saabs and BMW's we see all over? Well I saw this beat-up old Chrysler the other day and it had a bumper sticker that said Visualize Revolution."

I was cruising at 75, only ten over the speed limit, but I had to pay attention to the road. Two lanes south, two lanes north—they do get crowded down here around Kennebunk. There were things I wanted to talk to Wilson about before we got to Ogunquit, but they were still in motion in my mind, like a wheel of fortune still going around, slower and slower now, just about to stop...

"Evidently Michelle Boulanger and Jonathan Hall could be taken for twins," I said. "Not that it matters, but it's weird, huh?"

"So what did they pull? Bait and switch?"

"I don't know. Maybe. I'm not sure about the logistics, to tell you the truth."

And I wasn't sure about the navigation, either. We were about to get off at the Ogunquit exit, and I had no idea how to get to Bob Doucette's and Charles Sewell's house. The phone book I checked gave Ogunquit as their address. Very helpful.

"You know," Wilson said, "we could drop it."

I glanced over at her. She had lost all resemblance to a pit bull. In her red frame sunglasses with her red hair blowing in the breeze, she seemed much more like a mellow Irish Setter on a holiday.

"Look, Jo. Jonathan will testify that Peter was with him all night and the Night Owls will testify that they saw two short men go into his building on Bennett Street at one o'clock and one of them come out at one-thirty. Peter won't even be indicted. He's our client, Jo. We're not supposed to convict him."

"Clients aren't supposed to lie. To their lawyers or their detectives."

"And drivers aren't supposed to exceed the speed limit, either...You are taking this a little personally, don't you think?"

"Of course I'm taking it personally. How else am I supposed to take it? I don't care if he gets away with murder. I just hate being taken for a sucker."

Wilson didn't reply, but when I glanced over at her again, she was staring out the window with a grin on her face. "Tough guy," she said. And then in her own tough guy voice, "Nobody takes Jo Wilder for a sucker and lives. Nobody...You got the toll? Here, I've got change."

We negotiated our way off the turnpike and headed toward Route 1. I'd have to pull into the first gas station and start asking questions. Or wait until we got to Ogunquit and try the gay bar. If we could even recognize the gay bar.

"He was playing with us, Will. Every step we took, he was there ahead of us. The only thing that surprised him was Alzola showing up. He wasn't planning on that move. Everybody else had scripts."

"Then why did Peter send you to Peaks Island and forget to give Michelle the Dark her script? Or maybe she just didn't want a part in the play?"

I considered this, but I also had to pay attention to the road. Or not the road so much as the New York, New Jersey and Massachusetts drivers all over it. Summer in southern Maine can be trying.

"The Night Owls, Will, were not on homicide's witness list."

"So they missed somebody."

"Remember how George Smith insinuated that Ruiz had been killed by a faggot—or was a faggot and got killed while he was having sex? Remember?"

"Look, I'm willing to admit that it's beginning to sound like a lot of people were involved...maybe. Boulanger and company wanted Ruiz out of the way, and they orchestrated it, possibly with the assistance of our client. However, we have not been elected the local vigilante squad. Please keep that in mind."

I had to laugh, but I wasn't appeased. "So," Wilson continued in her brightest voice, "here we are in lovely Ogunquit. Let's just go to the beach."

"Why are you so into dropping this?"

"I've lost my killer instinct. Besides I read one of his poems."

"Whose?"

"Peter's. In that book of poems we got from Kenny Perkins."

"Jesus. So he knows Kenny Perkins, too? This is becoming..."

"Wait! There is such a thing as coincidence, you know. Solange's metaphysics notwithstanding."

"Well, my killer instinct is alive and well," I said, and pulled into a Ma and Pa's gas station.

"Bob Doucette's place?" The attendant knew it, just had to think a moment. "That'd be Parka Road."

And Parker Road? I was half expecting the classic native response to direction seekers: Parka Road? Well, you can't get there from here. (There and here being formed, in this case, of two syllables each.) But you could get there. Half a mile back down the road. Barn on your left. Take the next right. Bob's place was three quarters of a mile down. Duck pond in front. Can't miss the duck pond.

I'd expected Bob Doucette to own a beach house on Marginal Way in Ogunquit village, right on the water, but Parker Road was in the country. Pastures, fields, duck ponds, family graveyards, wild flowers. Peter had dragged us out here on purpose, as part of this psycho-drama he was directing. I knew it and it pissed me off. I was so pissed off that I was bound and determined not to notice how pretty it all was.

"Want to hear it? The poem?"

"No," I said. "I want to be able to go for his jugular without remorse."

I pulled into a driveway beside a duck pond in front of a red barn. The farmhouse was long, rambling, with a big front porch. Peter was sitting on the porch in a rocking chair just as though he had been expecting us.

"So," he said, getting up and holding out his hand to me as Wilson and I climbed the porch steps, "I guess you've been out to the island to see my friend Michelle."

Chapter 24

It was entirely different from what I expected. I expected a beach house and I got a farm. I expected defensiveness and I got graciousness. I expected to surprise him, but he had been expecting us for lunch.

He seemed so relaxed, so sincerely pleased that we had stopped in to visit... I almost fell for it, until he apologized for the public radio's afternoon selection. "I'll change it in a minute," he said. "*Gaiete' Parisienne* might not be the best musical accompaniment for this conversation."

And then, just to be sure we were with him, he added, "Maybe I should dig out a good somber Requiem. Though it's an awful nice day for a Requiem."

He was as smug as a spider inviting the flies into his parlor for tea.

Jonathan had gone to the village for some groceries but would be back any minute. Meanwhile what could he get us to drink?

Wilson leaned back in her rocker, looking like butter wouldn't melt in her mouth, and said, "Well, tell me, Peter, is this going to be a single shot conversation or a double? Or maybe a triple?" She had that gleam in her eye. She had picked up on something and now the game was afoot.

Peter just smiled languidly back at her. "Bob and Charles take their summer entertaining seriously. They have this bar on wheels... How about if I just wheel it out and you can direct me from there?"

It wasn't as though he didn't know how to choose his words.

As soon as he went inside the house, Wilson broke into one of her superb laughs.

"What?" I asked.

"I understand now. Why you're so rabid about this."

"Why am I so rabid?"

"Every sentence is a challenge."

"He wasn't like this last time. Of course he was acting last time."

"Well, the play's over now."

"Not really," he said, wheeling the port-o-bar onto the porch. "We're between the acts. Intermission. Unless you're working for BIDE, of course, or the Attorney General. I thought you were working for Gareth. Was I wrong?"

"No," Wilson said in her most spritely voice. "Not the Feds, not the state, but you yourself pay the freight, Mr. Lawrence. We've been hired by your attorney to gather information for your defense—period. This is just our way of reality checking. No more willing suspension of disbelief. It's time for the reviews."

"Wonderful. Constructive criticism is always welcomed."

They were both looking at me, and, in their own way, each of them was looking remarkably smug. "I'm taking into consideration the fact that you probably had to go off book pretty quickly," I began.

"Or that for many scenes there was no book to begin with," he said. "What's your pleasure here, ladies? They seem to have at least one variety of everything."

We got our drinks squared away, Wilson taking her Jack Daniels neat, I asking for rum and Pepsi, heavy on the Pepsi. One of us had to dig for truth, but one of us had to drive home. Peter was drinking Poland Spring water on the rocks.

Drinks in hand, we all leaned back in our rockers surrounded by pots of red and pink geraniums and waxed begonias, and I continued the review.

"When Ray Boulanger was busted last fall for trafficking in cocaine and marijuana, it was probably a given that the DEA would put the screws to him. They'd want the names of his distributors in exchange for a downward departure from the sentencing guidelines. This is their standard MO, trade a man twenty years of his life for his honor. But the Feds also gave him an alternative. They'd take his cocaine source. His marijuana network were his friends, but his coke connection was ready to carve up his family if he rolled, so Ray was in kind of a jam.

"You and Michelle must have started concocting this scheme as soon as Ray got busted and heard from Ruiz about what would come down if he rolled. You decided you had to kill Ruiz—that was the only way to get Ray out of a life sentence without endangering his kids or betraying his friends—but it had to be perfectly synchronized to coincide with Ray's proffer to the government. Because if Ruiz turned up dead before the U.S. Attorney approved the downward departure, Ray would have lost all his chips and there would be no deal at all.

"Somehow Michelle made contact with Ruiz and made arrange-

ments to meet him in Portland that Saturday night. You gave Ray the
go-ahead, and his lawyer set up the proffer meeting that Friday
afternoon, as late in the day as he could manage. Saturday night
Michelle meets Ruiz as planned, takes him to your apartment where
you're waiting for him. You kill him with the crystal. Michelle drives
home, you go back to Jonathan's. You wait five, six hours, until you
know Michelle is safely back in Washington County, and then you call
the cops. She's got an alibi. You've got an alibi. Ray's made his deal, and
José Ruiz is meeting his Maker."

"And I imagine it wouldn't be too difficult to lure Ruiz to a
meeting," Wilson added sweetly. "There was probably money owed
him. Probably quite a lot of money."

"Yes," Peter said, sipping his glass of water. "He lost his coke and
never got paid, poor guy. But please tell me how you deconstructed our
text. This is really fascinating... Oh, wait. Here's Jonathan. He'll want to
hear too."

A car pulled into the driveway, and Jonathan got out and started
up the path with an armful of bags. Peter vaulted over the porch railing,
gave Jonathan a kiss over his armful of bags, and went off to retrieve the
rest from the car. I'd never seen them together before. If I had, I guess
I would never have mistaken Michelle for Jonathan that night in
Deering Oaks. Standing beside him, she had made Peter seem like a
giant; next to Jonathan he was just a taller man.

Jonathan greeted us and went into the kitchen to unpack the bags.
It wasn't much like confronting killers. It's hard to think of killers
bringing in the groceries.

"I have to admit," Peter said, returning to his rocking chair, "when
Gareth told me he was hiring you two to do some investigative work,
I was pretty concerned. I knew you'd worked for Ray's lawyer so I
figured you'd put it together sooner or later. Especially because you've
got such a swell rep in town. Best P.I.'s in the state. I tried to talk Gareth
out of it, but he insisted. So we knew it was only a matter of time. Thank
God you don't work for the A.G.'s office."

"You mean, thank God we're not police dicks," Wilson said
grinning at him. Peter grinned back. He radiated warmth and friendli-
ness and I just couldn't see him, I still couldn't see him, bashing Ruiz's
head in with that damn amethyst crystal.

Then Jonathan joined us and pulled up a rocker and we were all
four together: a Penobscot, a Slav, a Celt and a WASP, four regular
North Americans rocking on a porch, critiquing a killing.

"I still have some questions," I said. "Small textual problems."

"Please," Peter said, waving his hand.

"Why did you cover your painting?"

"Ah, you noticed that, did you?"

"You pay us to notice things," Wilson said. I'd never quite thought of it like that before.

"Why did you think I covered the painting?"

"I couldn't figure it logically at all. To protect it, I assumed. But you must have planned to kill Ruiz in the bedroom all along."

Jonathan perked up at that like a good hound on the scent. "Wait a minute!" he said. "Peter..."

"It's OK, honey," Peter interrupted. "They're just deconstructing. Really, this is fabulous. So you went to the studio and you saw the painting covered. That made you suspicious. Did you notice anything else? About the sheet?"

"No," I said, wary now. "I guess I should have." He shrugged, but he was pleased about something. "The sheet puzzled us. And here's another question. Why did you let Michelle be seen with Ruiz? Someone might have recognized her."

"They had to meet somewhere and the sort of people who might recognize Michelle wouldn't be at a place like Gabriel's. That's one thing. Another is that she's a great make-up artist and so didn't look a whole lot like herself anyway."

"We got small, pretty, blonde female."

"Sort of generic, wouldn't you say?"

"It dispelled the gay angle, however."

"That was the idea. We wanted to dispel the gay angle. We wanted to divert it away from the gay scene entirely. Our intention was to make the setting and the characters entirely incongruous."

"Straight Latino killed in gay Indian's apartment," Jonathan said. "We wanted a little absurdity to creep in."

Wilson nodded to me. Yes, Peter, the setting had been just a tad problematic. Then she laughed out loud. "We had actively considered the possibility that the pretty blonde was Jonathan in drag."

"How sweet of you," Jonathan said, trying to sound demure. But Peter laughed hard, the way Wilson laughed. "That's really fabulous," he said. "That possibility never crossed my mind. Not once."

Wilson took over the deconstruction; Peter added ironies and serendipities. Like the fact that Ruiz's driver's license had Alzola's name on it. Much better to leave the body with a false ID like that, gratis, too, a gift of the gods, than with no ID at all. The mix-up gave Ray a couple of days' grace to get the government's motion granted before anybody even suspected that the dead man on Bennett Street was the very trafficker he was offering to the DEA. And like the fact that a friend visiting San Francisco had called Peter at Jonathan's at 2 AM Sunday morning, forgetting the time change, thus giving him another alibi, should he happen to need one.

"So," I said, feeling myself hardening against him again, "you've got alibis waiting in the wings. Don't you realize the more people involved in this conspiracy, the more chance you have of one of them ratting you out?"

"None of these people would rat me out. Why should they?"

"In a conspiracy to commit murder every member of the conspiracy is as guilty as the one who..."

"Yes, so they say. They love the charge of conspiracy, those servants of the most conspiratorial government on the face of the earth. But what does conspiracy mean? To breathe together. It's a nice image, isn't it? So we breathed together, and now one first class motherfucker won't be breathing down our necks anymore. We have a right to do this because the state's been falling down on the job. What possible justification is there for the establishment of a state to begin with if it isn't the protection of the people from invasion and civil disorder? Well, there's been an invasion and there's been civil disorder and this state hasn't done shit about it. In fact, I'd argue that the so-called war on drugs by escalating the street price of a harmless plant like hemp is directly responsible for an increased use of dangerous drugs, including alcohol, and for an increase in violence and other crimes against innocent people. We've had to take care of this criminal ourselves because they didn't give us a choice. But we were careful, we took precautions. Nobody involved knew more than was necessary to do his or her part. The most likely suspects will never need to lie while the ones who might need to lie will never be asked any questions. Artistically the construction is as crystalline as possible. We tried to write an absolutely clean, absurdist script. Everything moves between two poles: the incongruity between setting and character and the incongruity between victim and accused. Given those inconsistencies we thought an indictment would be unlikely and a conviction even more unlikely. The only wrinkle was you two. You could break the code. See, none of this is so incongruous or absurd to someone who knows that Zoe Neptune is my daughter, mine and Michelle Boulanger's."

"Exactly, Peter," I broke in. "Which is why I don't understand why you left that Father's Day card from her up on your bedroom wall. Why didn't you take it down?"

"I don't know," he said. "I thought of it. We cleaned the place up pretty well—no grass, no political stuff..."

"We got a little obsessional," Jonathan said. "We even defrosted the refrigerator."

"But I put Zoe's beautiful drawing up and then I just couldn't take it down. It kept reminding me why. We kept needing to be reminded why. All of us. Because monster slaying is generally reserved for heroes and we're all just regular, ordinary people, cast in roles not of our choosing..." His voice just died away, and he and Jonathan exchanged a look that was so private I couldn't begin to read it but so emotionally charged I felt its power move like a current between them. "Anyway," he said, addressing Wilson and me, "I'd like to say something to you in my defense."

"It isn't necessary," Wilson said. "You don't need to defend yourself to us. We're not under any obligation to report any of this to the AG. After all, Peter, we work for you."

"That's good, and we were counting on it, of course. But I have this monologue..."

"Be our guest then," Wilson said, waving her hand at him. He was, of course, irresistible.

Jonathan lit a cigarette. Wilson sipped her Jack Daniels. Peter studied his hands for a few seconds, getting into character, perhaps. I noticed a silver band on the ring finger of his left hand. Jonathan was wearing one just like it. How conventional, I thought. But it pleased me. After all, there was nothing else even vaguely conventional about this interracial homosexual marriage of theirs, this marriage of opposites— Jonathan so cute, blonde, mercurial; Peter so dark, brooding, intense, that Asiatic cast to his eyes, witness to his ancestors' trek across the ice from one continent to another. I was studying him so intently that he startled me by looking up right into my face.

"Maine is my home," he began. I was amazed at how he did this, stepped not out of character, but into it. This man who was speaking was Peter Lawrence. He was himself, only more so. He had taken his own personality and intensified it just the slightest so that all ambiguity, the sort of ambiguity we all carry with us, the ambiguity that makes us question ourselves and hesitate over words and fumble and scratch and smoke cigarettes, all that natural indecisiveness was purged away. This man, this Peter Lawrence, was just that fragment larger than life that if he wanted to sell cars for a living or con wealthy old ladies he'd be a rich man. "I was born here. My parents were born here. My mother's family back to before the European invasion lived on this land. I am a native and I feel a certain protectiveness, a guardianship, over this land. I don't take well to the idea of outsiders moving in and upsetting the natural ecology, physical and spiritual, of this place.

"But we all live with certain contingent realities: the laws and the punitive power of the state. There are laws in effect in this land which I am proud to ignore—not defy, but ignore—because they do not comprise part of my social contract with the state. The sodomy laws, for example, I would break on a daily basis if there were sodomy laws on the books in the state of Maine for me to break. I'm pleased that there aren't. The so-called controlled substance laws, which do exist here, I do break on a daily basis. I do not accept the premise that the state has a right to control the natural growth of plants nor what I may choose to do with those plants. If the state catches me growing a plant they consider illegal, an unlawful plant so to speak, and arrest the plant for being illegal and me for consorting with it, then I'm willing to take the consequences. The law is part of the reality I live with, and I'm not about to declare war on the state of Maine in defiance of that reality. Though I might join up if somebody else declared war... But that's another rap entirely.

"The cartel or the Mafia or whatever you want to call it, however...that is not an acceptable element in our reality here. It is not a tolerable element. It isn't indigenous, it isn't harmonious, it gives nothing, it only disrupts and destroys. We hope this little incident serves them with notice. They are not welcomed here, and they will not be tolerated here. We are armed and we are willing to fight to defend ourselves. Remember the Minutemen? Well..."

He was completely earnest, completely sincere...The next second he was grinning and had conjured up a joint from behind his ear. "Got a light, baby?" he said leaning over to Jonathan. "It still needs work."

"Don't worry about it," Jonathan said, lighting a match for him. "The real criminal will be tried and convicted and you'll never need to give your speech from the gallows. Thank God."

"Alzola you mean?" I said, taking the joint from Peter. "I wouldn't bank on it."

"Not Alzola. Alzola was so behind the scenes in this thing we didn't know anything about him until his name showed up on that license, and then he kidnapped you. Which scared the shit out of us, by the way..."

"We were going to call it quits," Jonathan said. "If you'd been hurt at all, the game was over."

"Did you buy the paper, Jon? I don't suppose you've seen the evening paper, Johannah? In good theatre, successful theatre, timing is everything. But this, this was more good luck than good management."

"They buried it on page five," Jonathan said, handing me a copy of the evening paper. "They must be so embarrassed." It was opened to page five. NARCOTICS COP CHARGED IN DRUG LORD'S SLAYING.

"Want me to read it out loud," I asked him, "or did you write the copy?"

"I'd love to hear it," Peter said. He was smoking the joint and looked as content as a pig in shit.

A state undercover policeman arrested Friday for possession and trafficking in LSD was charged today with the murder in Portland last week of a drug kingpin, the Attorney General's office announced this morning. Vincent Scully, an undercover law enforcer with the Bureau of Intergovernmental Drug Enforcement (BIDE), was charged with the murder of José Ruiz, a cocaine trafficker who was found bludgeoned to death last week in the home of Portland artist, Peter Lawrence. In announcing the new charges, a spokesman for the Attorney General revealed that Scully, a five year veteran of BIDE who worked on a number of major cocaine and marijuana arrests over the past year, may also have received large cash payments from dealers. Murder charges previously filed against Lawrence have been dropped.

"OK," Wilson said. "I'm lost."

Peter beamed at her. "You're in Ogunquit, and I'm about to open the champagne... Oh, and did you happen to notice that I'm not a gay activist anymore? Now I'm only a lowly Portland artist. How soon they forget."

Chapter 25

Peter popped the cork and filled three glasses with champagne, one with Poland Spring water. When we had all taken a glass and settled back in our chairs, he continued the deconstruction.

"Vince Scully showed up in town about eight months before Ray's bust. He dated Michelle's best friend up there, Andrea LaPlante, and moved in with her. He became part of the family. He was just as sincere and up front a guy as you could ask for. Post feminist on the cusp of New Age. Did more LSD than a merry prankster—or claimed to."

"Peter hated his guts," Jonathan put in. "Instantly. The moment they met."

"He struck me as a complete phony. But I thought he was a complete phony because he was after Andrea's pretty ass. It never occurred to me he was a narc."

"He was the one who set up the buy?" Wilson asked.

"He set up the buy all right—both ends of it. Hooked Ray up with the investor, Harold Connolly, BIDE agent, and with the supplier, José Ruiz, child-killer. Oh, not with Ruiz directly, of course. But he steered Ray in the right direction, gave him some leads, made some introductions. Aided, abetted and encouraged him every step of the way. Ray on his own wouldn't have had a clue how to deal on that level. That's the real crime here. And then what do they say to Michelle when she goes to the state for protection? Tough break, lady. Well, I say the state's got to eat that one... Cheers!"

"To the state eating it," Jonathan said, which was a toast we could all drink to.

"But wait," I said. "I understood that Ray had his own coke connection. That's what George Smith told me and Albert Greer. That Ray could bring in coke anytime..."

"Oh, right. `And the seas was fifty feet.'" Peter could lay on a good downeast accent all right; he sounded more like George than George did, "'And them winds were blowin' fierce. Then by God I look up...What do I see? The Coast Guard! Good lads, they've come to save us from the storm! But what's this now? They got them rockets pointin' right at us like you see in war shows, and they even sent one of them goddamn Aegis cruisers, what they got out to the Iron Works, made right here in this fair state with my fucking tax dollars. And so I holler out to 'em, Don't tread on me, motherfuckers!...' No, I love George and Albert. But when they start telling yarns... Ray probably thought he could bring coke in any time he wanted. But Ray's an old lobsterman smuggler hog farmer. Ray's not in the same league with José Ruiz. And since he's living in the same household with my daughter, I'm pretty thankful he's not."

"So you set Vince Scully up?"

"Not me. That's not my turf. But it was taken care of. They'll probably never get a murder conviction, but it'll be nice to see him in the hot seat for awhile. Better him than me.

"See, Scully made a big mistake. He shacks up with one of Ray's friends, eats at his table, gets high on his pot, and all the time the motherfucker's a spy for the state. Like what they used to tell us happened in Russia, right? State police spying on you, turning your kids into rat informers...remember all that? Well, that's our drug enforcement mentality, that's the model—Stalinist Russia. Anyway, so Vince pulled off this little charade, he should have scooted right back into the woodwork. But he was careless. Andrea tracked him down and convinced him that she didn't care if he was a moral degenerate pig, his body was so irresistible, and the asshole bought it. What amazing vanity."

Jonathan refilled our glasses. It was good champagne, cold and not too dry. I was intrigued by the way Wilson listened to Peter, by the way Jonathan watched him, by the difficulty I was having resisting him. He had conspired to kill a man, he had actually killed a man, in cold blood, and still I couldn't help feel that he was completely normal. He'd jump into Confucius' river to save a drowning child, no question. He'd probably even adopt it and take care of it. And I wasn't alone. Even Wilson, the totally fairminded, the absolutely just, even she seemed beguiled by him.

"Andrea lifted a few random but very personal items from Vince's house, and Michelle brought them along to my studio that night. Some she returned to Andrea with incriminating stains on them to plant at Vince's and some she left at my place for the cops to find. Absurd things, totally inexplicable, a collage of found items. That sheet over my painting, for example. At some point I would return to my studio and there would be my oil painting, still damp—it takes months for them to dry properly—covered with a sheet. I would go to the homicide detective berserk, demanding to know what asshole cop covered a wet painting with a sheet. And where did the damn thing even come from? It's not even one of mine. And it isn't. It's Vince Scully's, lifted right off his bed, got his body fluids all over it and his monogram at the corner. His mom always bought him monogrammed sheets."

I had to confess I hadn't noticed the monogram.

Andrea had also lifted a prescription bottle, a pair of sunglasses, and a penknife with Scully's initials engraved on it.

"Poor Vince," Jonathan said. "Always afraid of forgetting who he was."

"None of this would register until now," Peter said. "If the cops noticed at all, they'd assume V.S. was just another one of my boy friends."

"Of whom there are legions," Jonathan said.

"Legions," Peter repeated, smiling.

"And what would they find at Scully's house?"

"The contents of Ruiz's wallet. My front door key. And pounds of blotter acid. If you count the paper it's on, which they do. We have a friend who cooks up LSD like it was fried dough. And lots of money. Ruiz's money, in fact. Never let it be said that Ray Boulanger does not pay his debts."

Birds were chattering like crazy up in the big maple tree in the yard. The sun was in its early evening descent, though this close to the solstice it would stay light for hours and hours. Peter reached over to refill our glasses, but I didn't want any more. I couldn't tell what I felt, whether I was impressed or appalled.

"How could you do all this?" I asked him. I learned how I felt from the sound of my voice—appalled.

"But we didn't do it all," Peter said. "We hardly did any of it. Really all I did, for example, was provide the set. I was just a glorified property mistress."

"You don't call killing a man something?"

"I call killing a man something. Of course I do." His voice was gentle, completely serene. He had nothing to defend himself with, or he didn't want to defend himself anymore. "I've killed a man so I know that it's something. But I didn't kill José Ruiz. Like I said before—the most likely suspects have to be able to tell the truth. I was home with Jonathan until 4:45. I went to my studio, checked out the scene and came back at 5:15. My friend in San Francisco really did call at 2 AM, and I really did answer the phone. And I truly do not know who killed José Ruiz."

"You see," Jonathan said, "we were organized into cells, like revolutionaries. Or like affinity groups are organized in the Pledge of Resistance or ACT-UP or Clamshell or for any civil disobedience action. It's the same principle. Each group makes its own decisions by consensus, chooses its own target, does its own thing. Killing Ruiz wasn't our job. And except for Michelle, who was our contact, we don't even know who else was in that group."

Wilson sighed. I looked from Jonathan's face to hers. She gave me a big grin, and I realized I was bordering on euphoria. "He was dead when you got there," I said to Peter, stupidly. Happiness does make me incredibly stupid.

"Dead as a dodo," he said.

"And the crystal wasn't even your idea?"

"That had to be a collective act of sacrilege," Jonathan said, and he seemed euphoric too. "Those downeasters are such heathens."

"Setting up Scully, for example...we didn't have anything to do with that. We didn't need to. A lot of people were wicked pissed at that asshole."

"They probably held a lottery for that one," Jonathan said.

"And as for Ruiz...who dropped the rock on his head, how he came to be naked, who put the damn sheet on my painting..."

"Michelle. She'd think it so dramatically unlike you. Same with the amethyst, Peter. Amethysts," Jonathan said to us, "are getting to be talismanic for gay men these days. Michelle still has a little bit of rage left in her against all gay men, which comes out at odd moments. Like when she's bashing in heads, for example."

"I'm not sure a jury would get the complete significance in either case," I said.

Peter gave me a small smile. "No. Unless I really had a jury of my peers."

Jonathan got up and leaned over Peter and kissed him. "You're not going to need a jury of your peers. Or any jury. It's over, Peter."

It was like watching a window open up. Beyond the bravado and beyond the acting. A window onto fear and past the fear now, onto the most complete relief. I understood why Peter was telling us all this, what a catharsis it must be, how much they must need it.

"George or Albert," I said. "Two likely candidates."

"Maybe. But Ray has a mess of friends, and Michelle could marshall half the Penobscot nation if she wanted. All she needed up there with her was a guy with a good arm and an exquisite sense of timing."

"Meanwhile Alzola's going to get charged with that murder out in Bridgton," Wilson said. "Bob Freer. Know him?"

"No. But I know his best friend, Kenny Perkins. Good poet, Kenny. And a damn nice guy."

Jonathan refilled all our glasses. "Let's drink to love and to freedom," he said.

"To love and freedom," Peter said, raising his glass of bubbly Maine water. "Dare to struggle. Dare to win."

Chapter 26

They invited us for dinner and for some reason—hunger maybe—we decided to stay.

While the men cooked, Wilson and I took a walk down the road. At the end there was a path through some woods and then up to a slight rise. From the rise we could see across a field to marshes and dunes. The ocean was there, a few miles away.

It was getting onto evening, all the colors becoming muted, textured smooth and thick like velvet, and the shadows were long and the light magical, making every rock and leaf glow. The sky was a deep luminous blue in the east, magenta in the west. Birds of all musical persuasions were singing, chirping, cawing or whistling, and rabbits were feeding in the grass and the smell from the sea was thick and good.

"You haven't smoked a cigarette all afternoon," Wilson said. "Are you out?"

We hadn't said much to each other, so it was interesting that she should bring up smoking. We were crossing the field, and the fragrance of sweet grass and clover, mixed with an occasional bracing whiff from the sea, was making me delirious. I must have really been delirious because I said, "I quit."

"You quit? Smoking? You? When?"

"Today. Just now."

"Oh," she said.

"I've smoked enough cigarettes," I said. "I'm going to let things get out of control. I'm testing my courage."

The colors and sounds and textures of the world were already out of control, very close, moving in closer by the minute. When I don't smoke, the world becomes more of a living presence. There's no smoke screen between us anymore. It scares the daylights out of me.

"It's nice out here," she said.

We walked for awhile just breathing together. Then she said, "I'm sure glad I'm not a cop anymore."

"Are you?"

"Yes."

"Why, Will?"

"I always liked Robin Hood better than the Sheriff of Nottingham. Didn't you?"

"But won't this keep you up nights? You're a terrible moralist, Will."

"This won't keep me up nights. I promise. How about you?"

"No. But I'm glad Peter didn't kill him. I am glad about that."

"He wanted a clean script. Simple plot. Few actors. I don't know if I buy that affinity group stuff. I mean, myself, if I were going after somebody for threatening my kid, I'd want to do the job myself."

"Maybe that's exactly the way Michelle felt. Maybe they drew straws." But I remembered the amazing light inside his paintings and the card from Zoe Neptune on the wall and Jonathan's frantic voice on the phone. "Besides, I don't think he could have killed someone like that. Not like that. He's a warrior. He'd fight it out, man to man. And frankly, I don't think Jonathan would have let him do it. I think Jonathan has a pretty heavy investment in Peter's mental health. Anyway, I hope we were an appreciative enough audience."

"We were the perfect audience. An audience of his peers. Like an audience of other actors. And think of it! We're the professionals and those uppity amateurs stumped us. How could you have missed the monogram on that sheet?"

"I knew the damn sheet was important...Well, Vince Scully's sure going to be sorry he messed with that crew."

"There's karma for you. That's the kind of karma I understand. You fuck someone over one month, you get fucked over in return the next. Simple cause and effect and you don't have to wait ten lifetimes to see it operate."

We came to the water's edge, a marshy riverbank. The river itself was mirror-still, and you could see in it a perfect reflection of the sky above and the oyster shell pink clouds sailing in the sky and even the cattails on the banks. The air was filled with wild sound from crickets and frogs and birds. On the other side of the river were the dunes, and on the other side of the dunes was the sea. We both stood there, dumbfounded, as though we'd never seen the Atlantic Ocean before.

"Ogunquit Beach," she said finally. "You can't get there from here."

"Jonathan said there's a footbridge about a mile or two down."

"Want to take a walk?"

"What's the other option?"

"Poetry reading?... I know it's only been a day, but have you given any thought to...anything?"

"Yeah," I said. "I've been thinking about it."

"Well, don't yell 'yes' too loud, Wilder, because I have very sensitive ears... I want to read this to you, OK?"

It was OK, not that she waited for me to say so. She was carrying the book in her jacket pocket and whipped it out like it was her 9mm. There was a convenient log by the riverside, and we sat on it and let ourselves exist in that radiant western light sinking behind us bathing everything in gold. And Wilson read:

> *When the two brothers, Monster Slayer and Child Born of Water,*
> *came to their father, the Sun, he had them swallow jet and turquoise*
> *to give them courage and the strength to fight the monsters of the*
> *earth.*

Nothing else frightens you
   not retroviruses
   or neo-nazis
   or warnings from the surgeon general.
No, you don't live in terror of environmental holocaust
   or lose sleep over that billboard on 95
   DANGER. SEABROOK NUCLEAR ZONE
         NO EVACUATION POSSIBLE.
Nothing scares you
   not high places
   or dark alleys
   not even the rising cost of Kodak paper,
Nothing, nothing, except that you might be happy.
   Ah, the fear of happiness,
   that you might have been chosen for this over others,
   swallowed it down one morning with your cereal like the
        prize in the box.
And now, lurking around the corner,
   long life and felicity
   a green road ahead,
   no monsters in sight.
Listen, this sweet darkness, canopy of stars,
It's a gift, like our bodies, your body, mine.
Look, it's a gift, this sky, this earth,

That our lips touch, our tongues.
A long shot, really, that we're here at all,
Born with those bits of jet and turquoise stuck in our throats.
But it's true, my brother, you've swallowed them down and now
It's just too late to be afraid.
You have fallen into happiness
    and kissing me—can't you see it?—
    you are like a man swimming with dolphins
    still telling himself he should be scared
    going out so far beyond his depth.

⁊ ⁊ ⁊

"He's got a good voice," I said after some time had elapsed. "You have a good voice, too. But the poet's voice. I mean, it's...well, I like it."

Pretty lame, Wilder. But Will just said, "Good."

"Maybe Jonathan and I should start a support group for the emotionally terrified."

"Jonathan looks like he's doing OK."

"He does, doesn't he?...You know, of course, that the emotionally terrified need rock solid commitments preferably written in blood."

"I know. I brought my knife."

"Oh, Will," I said, so moved that she had thought to bring her knife that I threw my arms around her and practically knocked her over. "I really love you."

Holding her, I inhaled a stunning blend of Shalimar and sour mash whiskey and felt the bulge of a poetry book in one pocket and a pistol in the other. Her hair was burnished by the long rays of the sun; she was as solid as goodness and as warm as the light on my back.

"Is that something like a 'yes'?" she asked.

And I said yes, something like a yes, and yes, the answer is yes, and yes, of course, yes.

⁊ ⁊ ⁊

The grand jury that met before Bastille Day indicted Vince Scully for the murder of José Ruiz. Wilson and I caught the next available flight to Lisbon and spent two weeks in bed with occasional forays out into the night to listen to fado music and drink green wine (and white wine and red wine). We even ventured forth by day to lie around topless on the beaches of the Algarve. Wilson loved the church filled with bones and the Moorish castle with the Christian graveyard inside; I loved the music best.

Months later Scully was tried on the murder charge. The trial ended in a mistrial; there was a hung jury. Andrea LaPlante appeared as a witness for the defense. Her testimony that Scully had called her the night of the murder from his father's house in Caribou, along with other inconsistencies in the prosecution's case, was enough to deadlock the jury. After all, he was a cop.

The players had evidently re-written the final scene and decided to let the fall guy off the hook.

In the end the murder of José Ruiz sullied forever the record of the Portland Police Department. To this day it remains unsolved.

Enrique Alzola wasn't as lucky as Vince Scully. They couldn't pin Bob Freer's murder on him, but they didn't really need to. He was convicted of trafficking in cocaine. Thirty years—and he didn't get a downward departure.

As for us—ah, that first person plural!—we have not decorated our office in crystals, but Wilson did give me an earring of Artemis, the Amazon goddess, with a tiny amethyst stone in her arrow tip. To remind you you've got the hottest profile in town, she says.

What she means is, To remind you you're a slayer of monsters. To remind you have fallen into happiness and it's too late to be afraid.

We didn't even have to get ourselves a dog.

Agnes Bushell was born in Queens, New York, in 1949, attended the University of Chicago and the University of Southern Maine. A long-time activist for social justice in the United States and abroad, she has worked as a paralegal and as an instructor of writing and literature at the Maine College of Art and the San Francisco Art Institute. She is the author of *Local Deities* and an earlier Johannah Wilder mystery, *Shadowdance*. While maintaining a residence in Maine, Bushell is currently living in Berkeley, California.

Look for these other quality books from Astarte Shell Press:

Keep Simple Ceremonies edited by Diane Eiker and Sapphire. This rich addition to the emerging genre of feminist rituals celebrates our life passages, friendships and political commitments. 150 pages • $12.95

Girl to Woman: A Gathering of Images by Susan Hauser. An eloquent memoir of growing up in northern Minnesota, in language that is meditative, hilarious, grief-filled and evocative. 126 pages • $10.95

Celebrating Ourselves: A Crone Ritual edited by Edna M. Ward. This powerful community ritual has evolved over ten years of honoring the passage into old age of twenty-four women. Developed in the Feminist Spiritual Community of Portland, Maine, it is a moving celebration of that passage. 50 pages • $6.00

Vision and Struggle: Meditations on Feminist Spirituality and Politics by Eleanor H. Haney. Rooted in a commitment to social, economic and ecological justice, the author develops a normative framework for feminist theology and ethics. 150 pages • $10.95

The Moon in Hand: Journeys into Feminist Mysticism by Eclipse. Through meditation, stories, prayers and rituals on each of the four directions, this book invites us on a powerful, ecstatic and wrenching journey into the heart of the ancients, the earth and ourselves. 154 pages • $12.95

Feminism for the Health of It by Wilma Scott Heide. Essays by a renowned activist for racial justice, nurse and third president of NOW. 164 pages • $6.95

A Feminist Legacy: The Ethics of Wilma Scott Heide and Company by Eleanor H. Haney. An intimate portrait of Wilma Scott Heide, a founding mother of the current feminist movement, activist, humorist and scholar. 208 pages • $8.95

For a complete catalog of the books offered by Astarte Shell Press write:
Astarte Shell Press
P.O. Box 10453
Portland, Maine 04104